The Dullahan

Copyright © 2023 by Alex Khan

All rights reserved.

No part of this publication may be reproduced, distributed, or transmitted in any form or by any means, including photocopying, recording, or other electronic or mechanical methods, without the prior written permission of the publisher, except as permitted by U.S. copyright law. For permission requests, contact [include publisher/author contact info].

The story, all names, characters, and incidents portrayed in this production are fictitious. No identification with actual persons (living or deceased), places, buildings, and products is intended or should be inferred.

Book Cover by Alerim

Edited by Joseph Nassise

*To those who believed in me -
Thank You*

Chapter 1

The ring of a church bell reverberates through the air. I look around to find myself in the middle of what looks to be a Renaissance fair. Medieval buildings lay side to side along a single long dirt road. The sun is setting in the distance, the cloudy sky turning purple as a result. The church bell continues to ring, seemingly growing louder as blood rushes to my ears. I begin to walk cautiously down the road stretched out before me. As I walk, a rotten smell fills my nose.

Jesus Christ that reeks!

A roar of fury echoes around before being cut short by a scream of pain. I start to pick up the pace, jogging down the dirt road. The road begins to twist and curve aggressively as it becomes narrower. The buildings on either side of me grow bigger, towering over me and blocking out any sunlight that remained. Just as the claustrophobia begins to set in, the road opens into a large square.

The square is littered with bodies. People in merchant and peasant clothes lay strewn about, their bodies all but cut in half. Across the square I see a horse-drawn carriage. The rotten smell in the air is more potent than before. The horses themselves were covered in green, rotting flesh.

In the center of the square is a large fountain. Next to it, I see my cousin, Brian, cowering in fear with his back pressed against the fountain. Looming over him is a large figure, wearing all black and holding a long whip.

"And so, your time has come, Brian, son of Arthur. Have you any last words?" The large figure's voice is deep and full of malice.

"Why?" Brian groans, "why are you doing this?"

The figure does not answer. Instead, a flash of blinding white light explodes before me, heat emitting from it. I shield my eyes from the light until it subsides. When I look back at my cousin, I am startled to see the figure is now facing me. With the sunlight fully gone from the sky now, all I can see is his outline.

"Aaron Ward," he says, "In time, you will face the same fate. Be prepared, for the Dynasty of Burke's end is neigh!"

The air around me seemingly explodes with wind, forcing me off my feet. The wind slams me into the side of a building behind me, holding me in place inches off the ground. I force myself to look in the direction of the dark figure before me. And it's then that I see the man is missing his head!

"See you soon, Aaron, son of David…"

***

I feel something bounce off my shoulder. The sudden sensation startles me, and I jump up in a panic, nearly falling out of my chair. The other students around me all start to laugh and I frantically look around, disoriented. My eyes eventually lock with those of my teacher, Mr. Cray. He glares a me with disappointment.

"Mr. Ward," he says, his voice high pitched and nasally, "While I am well aware that this is the last day of school for the year, I find it very disrespectful when my students fall asleep in my class."

"Sorry, Mr. Cray." I rub sleep out of my eyes. "I wasn't trying to be rude."

Mr. Cray sighs, "I expect better Aaron. I hope this will not be a problem after summer break is over."

I look to my left to see my friend, Zoë, giggling at me from a few desks away. I smile weakly at her before looking back to Mr. Cray.

"Absolutely not, sir. I promise it won't happen again."

"Good." Seeming satisfied, Mr. Cray turned back to the whiteboard at the front of the classroom, "Now as I was saying…"

His voice fades into the background as I cautiously reach for my phone. As I tap on the screen, I see I've got a few texts from Zoë. Checking them, I see a picture of me sleeping, followed by a caption that reads: **Bring back naptime at school**

I chuckle at the lame joke before replying. I ask her if she wants to do something after school. It doesn't take half a minute for her to reply, asking if I want to go to the aquarium. I, of course, say yes.

Satisfied with that, I start to think back on the wicked nightmare I just had. I've had quite a few in my life, of course, but never one so vivid. So real.

What was Brian doing there?

I try to shake it off, but it isn't until I hear the school bell ring that I'm able to do so. Zoë meets me at my desk as the other students all rush out of the classroom. Mr. Cray shouts after them all to no avail. With the last class of the day finally over, summertime officially begins. And until next September, what Mr. Cray has to say doesn't matter to anyone.

Zoë looks down at me, playful curiosity glimmering in her eyes, "So, what were you dreaming about?"

"Nothing, just some crazy nightmare." I rub sleep out of my eyes.

"I figured; you were thrashing about like you were in a strait jacket."

"Guessing that's what caught Mr. Cray's attention?" I get up from my desk and start to walk towards the door, Zoë in tow.

"Yep. Should've been recording. You know he threw a whiteboard eraser at you?"

"Oh, so that's what that was," I say, chuckling.

"Yep." We stop walking as we reach her locker. Why she even bothered bringing anything with her to school on the last day was beyond me. I lean against the neighboring locker as she collects her things and take a moment to just look at her.

Zoë is my best friend and neighbor. Although I have always wished for her to be something more, I know that I would never gain the courage to confess my feelings for her. She is beautiful yet terrifying in many ways. Platinum blond hair, steel gray eyes, and the body of a model, yet she is no mere damsel. She is a true punk, dressed in the classic torn black jeans, with an Alkaline Trio t-shirt underneath a black plaid shirt. A dream and a nightmare all in one.

"So," she slams her locker shut, "ready?"

"Aquarium, right?" I ask.

"Yep, you're driving."

"Who else?" We chuckle at that as we make our way towards the exit of the school.

As we both step outside, I take a moment to look back at the front of the school. The building is big and nice, with a modern design. Although I was glad to be free from it, a sad realization sinks in.

Next year is the last year.

After that, it's onto the rest of our lives. Course, I still had no idea what the rest of my life was going to be like. College? Trade schools? Life as a Hobo? I truly have no idea what I'll be doing a week from now, let alone two years. Zoë and I reach my car and she opens the back door, causing a bunch of robotics junk to fall out.

"Jesus Aaron!" Zoë laughs, "You need to clean your car out. The robotics competition was nearly two months ago."

"Yeah, yeah, I know. Just haven't gotten around to it yet," I groan as I help her pick up all the junk and throw it back in my car along with her bag. "Besides, half this shit is yours, too."

"Um, no," Zoë chuckles, "the pile of crap I got in my garage is mine. All this in here is your problem."

"Whatever." I sigh. I start the engine and proceed to leave the school.

"Jeez granny, gonna go any slower?" Zoë provokes.

"We're in a school zone."

"So?"

I laugh. *Oh, she wants me to go faster huh?* I press my foot down harder on the gas pedal, and my car takes off. Zoë cheers as we leave the school in our dust.

***

Zoë and I are standing in the tunnel of the aquarium. Fish of all different types swim overhead, along with a pair of sea turtles. Zoë takes a deep breath and I watch as her shoulders relax, a smile spreading across her face.

"God, I love it here," she says. "I feel so at peace. Like, nothing matters here. It feels so free."

"Even though nothing here is?" I mock.

"Oh, shut up, you know what I mean," Zoë rebukes.

"Yeah, I hear ya."

We come here all the time. This being Zoë's favorite place means that we have spent a lot of time here. We've seen all the exhibits dozens of times, yet it's always the first place on her mind whenever we want to go do something. I don't mind, it's nice here. Of course, right now I'm not paying as much attention to the sea-life. I'm just looking at Zoë. My stomach twists and my heart compels me to tell her how I feel. But I don't.

Why ruin the moment? What if she doesn't feel the same? Then not only is today ruined, but maybe all of the summer, too.

I feel my phone start to buzz in my pocket. Just as I go to pull it out, Zoë starts for the exit of the tunnel, "Come on! I wanna go see the dolphin exhibit."

"Ok, let's go." Forgetting all about my phone, I race off after her.

As we make our way to the dolphin exhibit, I find my mind drifting back to my dream. *Why can't I stop thinking about it?* The part about Brian especially is what sticks to me as Zoë and I walk. A chill runs up my spine just thinking about it. I feel the urge to call him and check on him. After all, it has been a while since we've talked. Not since his dad died, something he and I have in common.

I pull my phone out, ignoring the missed call from my sister, and start to call Brian. The phone rings for a while before I finally get a voicemail. I tell him that I was just calling to check in and want to hear back from him. As I hang up the phone, I see that Zoë has pulled farther ahead of me as we both near the dolphin exhibit.

I jog to catch up to her, just in time to see a dolphin explode out of the water, doing a flip in midair before sinking once more into the pool. Zoë and I lean against the guard railing and watch the dolphins for a while in silence. Some women, who I assume work for the aquarium, come out and starts making the dolphins do tricks for food.

The crowd of people around me cheer as the tricks continue. But after a while, I've had enough. I tell Zoë I want to get going and with a slightly disappointed look on her face, she nods in agreement.

As we make our way to the exit of the aquarium, out of the corner of my eye I see two dark shadowy figures just to the right of the doors. Just as I turn my head to look at them, they disappear. I look around, hoping to see where they went, but am disappointed if not shocked to find that there is no one remotely near the spot they were a moment ago.

"Aaron?" Zoë asks, directing my attention towards her, "you good?"

"Yeah," I lie, "yeah, just thought I saw something."

"Man, you must really be tired. How late did you stay up last night?"

"It's nothing," I brush her off, "just seeing things I guess."

"Whatever dude." She shrugs.

We arrive back at my car and Zoë, once more, throws her bag in the back seat. As we start to drive out of the parking lot, I find myself fixated on the spot where I saw the two figures. *What is going on with me today?*

***

I pull into my driveway, noticing as I do that my mom's car isn't there. Zoë sighs, her head going limp against the headrest. I sit in silence for a moment with her, just relaxing.

"Ya know," Zoë turns her head to face me, "I have a good feeling about this summer."

"Oh, and how's that?"

She smiles. "Simple, me and you are gonna do a lot of shit. For starters, Deacon wants to hang out soon."

"Oh, come on, Zoë!" I groan.

"What?"

"How many times do we have to go over this. I hate that guy."

"You barely know him!" she groans.

"I know enough not to like him. A guy his age hanging out with highschoolers is creepy enough as is. Not to mention-"

"He isn't that much older than us," Zoë cuts me off. "Besides, I like him. He's nice, funny, gets us alcohol."

"Yeah, a twenty-something guy hanging out with two highschoolers getting them drunk definitely isn't sketchy at all."

"Look, whatever." Zoë gets out of the car, and I rush to follow her, "I like him. He's as much my friend as you are, so you need to just get over that."

"So, what? You'd pick him over me?"

"I didn't say that!" she snaps. "God, Aaron, every time I mention him, you freak out."

"I just don't trust the guy. I'm sorry if you don't get the same feelings, even if it's concerning that you don't." I stop and take a deep breath, choosing my words carefully.

8

"Look, even if you trust the guy, even if you love him, as your friend, it's my job to look out for you and tell you when something is off."

Zoë takes a deep breath as well before continuing, "I know... And I appreciate that. But Aaron, I am a big girl. I can look after myself. Now I'm going to be hanging out with him later this week, and I'd really love it if you'd come with me."

I clench my jaw in frustration. *Why does she need me with her if she trusts him so much?*

"Aaron?" Zoë takes a few steps forwards, taking my hand in hers, "Please?"

I cave, "Fine. But the second he starts talking about smoking or drinking, we're leaving."

"God, you're such a buzz kill!" Zoë chuckles. "Fine, I promise."

She releases my hand and I feel a pang of sadness. I watch as she slowly starts to walk backwards towards her house before she stops and turns around. "Hey, I love you. You know that right?"

In the brotherly way. Not the way I'd prefer.

"Yeah, I know." I smile weakly. "I love you, too."

With that, she smiles and turns away.

I watch her go for a moment before following her lead and walking inside my own house. As the door slams beside me, I feel the silence and emptiness around me.

I assume Jake is with Chloe. It's unusual for the house to be so quiet, though. Normally either my mom is home doing dishes or watching her reality shows, or Chloe is running around taking care of her son, and my nephew, Jake. That kid really makes her work, but I know she loves him. And she knows both my mom and I are always willing to help when we can.

I head to my bedroom and flop down on my bed. The room itself was nothing special. Average size, with alternating grey and blue walls and a dirty old carpet. Clothes are strewn about the floor from the past few days. My tv hangs on the wall opposite my bed, and in between sits a small, worn-down leather recliner. My game console rests on a table beneath the tv, ready to be used to play whatever rushed/overpriced game I got my hands on next.

Still feeling tired, I decide that today is not the day to be cleaning. Instead, I peel off my socks and scratch at the deep lines they leave in the sides of my ankles.

Ahh, bliss.

I lay back on my bed, my head sinking into my pillow. Sleep threatens to take me but then my phone rings. This time, I answer it, seeing that it is my mom

"Hey, Mom," I answer.

"Are you home yet?" she asks me.

"Just got home, yeah, where is everyone?"

"Honey, I'm sorry to tell you this over the phone…" I can hear in her voice that she's very upset about something.

"Tell me what, Mom?" I sit up on my bed. "What happened?"

"It's your cousin, Brian." The mention of his name sends a shiver down my spine. "Honey, he passed away."

Suddenly, the nightmare I had earlier scared me a whole lot more. I was more scared than I ever thought I could be, in fact.

Chapter 2

I stand over my cousin, Brian, with barely any air in my lungs. It's hard to see him like this, all trussed up in a fancy suit, with his hair slicked down and his skin pale as paper. The mortician tried to cover the numerous scars on his face, but to no avail. They show through the makeup as clear as ever. Brian was only twenty-four, yet he looked nearly forty; with gray hairs and wrinkles all over, he was almost unrecognizable.

What happened to you?

I think back to the days when I was a kid, before I entered high school. Brian was a senior and was as happy as could be. He had shaggy, sandy, brown hair and a chiseled jaw with the lightest facial hair on his chin. He certainly knew how to have fun and people loved him for it. He always had a way with knowing what was going on in your head, which for me at the time was most likely either basketball or video games. He always made me feel wanted.

"Aaron?" asks a soft voice.

I turn around and see my sister, Chloe, beautiful as ever, her red hair wrapped in a bun; her pale blue eyes piercing through me. She wore a simple black dress, with a pearl necklace she probably borrowed from my mom.

"Aaron, are you feeling ok?"

"I'm fine, just haven't slept the last few nights."

"Aaron!" Her eyes light up with concern. "That's not good."

"I know, I know," I say, "but it's not something I can really control."

"That's normal I guess," she sighs, "but promise me you'll get some sleep tonight!"

"I promise."

Of course, I haven't told anyone the details of the nightmare I had. I can barely believe it myself; I doubt anyone else would. The dream is the main reason I haven't slept the past few days. I've been too freaked out to let myself.

"Anyways, we should get back to our seats. The service is about to begin," Chloe says.

I nod in agreement and follow her back to our seats. As we sit down, I notice Chloe's son, Jake, is playing a game on her phone. Chloe is only twenty-two, she had Jake near the beginning of her senior year of high school. A stupid mistake she made with some jackass who didn't want to use a condom. Of course, nobody really minds. Jake is a sweet kid and having him around the house certainly lifts everyone's spirits and Chloe is a natural mom. Jake has short dark brown hair and hazel eyes. He is dressed in a cute little blue suit. According to my mom he looks exactly like my dad did at that age.

As the priest begins the eulogy for Brain, I think back on Brian and his life. He had practically been a big brother to Chloe and me. He was always looking out for us in school and keeping Chloe safe from the horde of assholes who chased after her. That is until his dad died a few years ago, after which he became a shut in. He almost never went outside or spent any time with us. I knew something was wrong, and after seeing the scars on his face, it seems I was right.

I look around the funeral home and see dozens of people, many of whom I don't know. Some I assume are distant family I haven't met yet or have forgotten. Others are probably friends or some other form of relations.

Everyone seems truly saddened at the loss of Brian, with a few people wiping tears away and others listening acutely to the priest's speech.

"...and now, I believe Brian's cousins would like to speak," the priest calls out. "Aaron and Chloe Ward, would you join me up here please?"

I make my way up to the front of the room alongside my sister. We begin to talk about how great a guy Brian was. Or Chloe does, as I can't seem to bring myself to speak.

"I often think of the time Brian was my date to my first homecoming dance," Chloe chuckles. "He said it was because he didn't trust anyone at my school to keep me safe." The audience laughs, eager for a chance to smile on this dreary day. Chloe goes on to talk about how much she will miss Brian. How much she'll miss his smile, his obsession for baseball, how his clothes always looked like he had fought a bear three minutes ago, and so on.

As Chloe continues, I scan the crowd of people around me. My gaze falls on an ancient but tall woman. Her short gray hair is tightly tied in a bun underneath a large black funeral hat. She seems almost lost, staring blankly at the ceiling. As I watch her, she suddenly snaps her head in my direction, her face contorting in fear. We lock eyes and for a moment, terror grips me. As we stare at each other, the look of fear on her face melts away into sadness.

What are you staring at?

"Aaron?" I hear Chloe ask.

"Huh?" Startled, I realize that I've just been standing silently in front of the audience. "Sorry, it's uh," I can't seem to get the words out.

"It's ok, this is hard for everyone," the priest interjects.

"Yeah," I nod, taking a deep breath. "I don't really know what to say. Growing up, I didn't have a lot of friends, let alone a brother to follow around and bother. But then Brian started to hang out with me. He looked after me and made me feel welcome." I pause, smiling as I remember a story. "I remember this one day, just after school, I'd gotten beat up by a couple of kids. While my mom freaked out and talked to the teachers, Brian just decided to teach me how to fight. For the next week or so, that's all we did. Because of Brian, I stopped getting picked on in school. I think that was the first time I started thinking of him more as a big brother than my cousin." I pause, looking around the room. I see my mom and my Aunt Katrina, Brian's mom, crying together.

"I don't know what life is gonna be like without him around." I look up and direct my attention to the old lady once again, who continues to stare at me, a single tear falling down her cheek. "But I do know this, I will miss him as much as a brother can. I hope that one day, he and I will see each other again."

With that, the priest continued speaking as Chloe and I went back to our seats. Once we sat down, my mom leans over to us.

"That was very nice, kids. I'm sure Brian would've appreciated that."

"Of course, Mom," Chloe responds in a choked-up whisper.

My mom is an older version of my sister, with long, red hair that rests gently on her shoulders. Her skin is pale, and she has light blue eyes. Today she wore a simple black dress. I have been told I look more like my dad than my mom, with short, thick, dark hair and a lanky build. My skin has a nice tan from my days outdoors with my friends. If it weren't for Jake, I'd have stuck out like a sore thumb sitting by both girls.

The eulogy went on for a while after Chloe and I spoke. Afterwards, when it was over, it was time to leave for the cemetery. As I made my way out, I was distinctly aware of someone watching me.

***

I've always hated funerals. I had been to too many growing up, including my dad's when I was five. They were always depressing and watching Brian's casket was lowered into the ground was even more so. I look up and see Aunt Katrina in tears, barely held up by my mom as she sobs into her arms. I find it hard to watch and look around desperate for something to distract me from the burial.

As I look behind me, I see the old lady again. She is standing just a few feet away and while everyone else is either looking to the ground or the grave, she is staring right at me. Her eyes are cloudy and her face emotionless.

What is her deal?

I hear a dull *THUD* as Brian's casket hits the bottom of the grave. I turn back to see my aunt step forwards and drop a single flower on top of it. People begin to do the same, walking away afterwards. As the crowd disperses, I look to my left to see Chloe and Jake.

Chloe looks at me, "Well, it's finally over."

"Yeah, thank God," I reply, my voice hollow.

"Can we go now?" Jake asks.

I chuckle at him. Jake was a typical kid, full of energy and with no patience. And like any kid, he probably found funerals incredibly boring. Maybe if he'd known Brian more, he'd be sadder. If that was the case, I'm glad he didn't. One less sad day in his life.

"Sure, thing goofball, let's give Grandma and Aunt Katrina a few minutes, okay?" Chloe asks.

As Chloe and Jake make their way to the car, I start to look around for that strange old lady. I can't see her anywhere, so instead I find my mom. She is standing over Brain's open grave alongside my Aunt Katrina. I begin to walk towards them and catch them talking.

"I just don't understand, why does this keep happening?" I hear my aunt sob into my mom's arms.

"I don't know Kat. I wish I did," my mom says, consoling her.

They stand there in silence for a moment, broken only by my aunt's sniffling. I truly feel bad for her. She has suffered a lot of loss in her life, first her husband and now Brian. Now with him gone, I don't know what she'll do.

What did she mean by this keeps happening?

"Sorry to interrupt," I finally say, "but everyone is already starting to leave for our house." They look at me; my mom's eyes are sad and tired, while my aunt's eyes are puffy and pink.

"Oh, hi Aaron," my aunt says weakly. "Sorry, I just-"

"No, don't be sorry," I stop her. "You have every right to grieve. I just wanted to make sure nobody got left behind."

"Thank you, honey." My mom smiles. She turns to my aunt, "Let's go Kat, you shouldn't be alone right now."

My aunt nods her head and follows her as we begin to walk to the car. As we do so, I can't help but think of that old lady.

"By the way, who was that really tall, old lady?" I ask.

My mom turns and looks at me, her expression a mix of emotions. "Um, what old lady?"

"That really tall lady who stood behind me during the burial," I replied. "I also saw her during the eulogy. She seemed kinda confused or something."

I watch as my mom's face contorts in anger before she shakes it off. "Oh, that's just your Great Aunt Claudia. She is one of your dad's relatives." I want to press further, but I can tell my mom isn't happy with the topic, so instead we finish the walk in silence.

***

As we pulled into our driveway, I see Jake running around in circles in the front yard. As I step out of the car, I hear him screaming my name.

"Uncle Aaron!"

I walk over to see cookie crumbs on his face.

"Uncle Aaron, can you please play with me?" Jake begs.

"Well, it sounds like you are in desperate need of some fun." I give him a wide smile. "So, what do you want to play?"

"Hmmmmm…" Jake ponders. After a moment of deep thought, he finally opens his mouth in a wide, grin. "I wanna play cops and robbers."

"Oh no, you know your mom doesn't like that game." I shake my head.

"Please!" he shouts.

I hold my ground by shaking my head, but he doesn't give up.

"PLEEEEEEEEEEEEEASE!" he hollers.

I can't help but smile.

"Fine." I chuckle. "How about this? You run and hide, and I count to twenty. When I'm done 'Detective Aaron Ward of the CPD' is comin for ya!'" I give him my best gruff cop voice.

"Yay!" Jake cheers.

"One, two, three…" I continue to count as Jake runs away around the house. When the time is up, I chase after him. We play cops and robbers for about fifteen minutes, and I chase him around long enough to tire him out. When that happens, I lead him inside and find Chloe waiting.

She greets me with a toothy smile, "Thanks for that, Aaron. The little goofball can really wear me out."

"No problem, always happy to help out with the," looking at Jake and switching into my gruff cop voice, "meanest outlaw in all of Chicago."

Jake giggles and Chloe pouts, "Oh really. That's what you did with him?"

"It's not my fault," I plead, "the little dude wouldn't take no for an answer."

Chloe lets out a defeated sigh, "Ok, just tell me you weren't rough on him."

"Of course not. I just chased him around the house a little."

Chloe seems to accept this as good enough. After some meaningless small talk, I head for the kitchen and grab a glass of water. Sitting down at the table, I take a deep breath.

Jake really tired me out.

As I sit at the kitchen table, members of my family gather throughout the house, trying their hardest to not talk about Brian. You'd think it would be hard to do, but with how frequently my family members die, people start to get used to it. Hell, at this point I was so used to attending funerals that I could just shut off my brain and the day would fly past me, just like school.

My first funeral was my dad's. I was young when he died, so I guess that helped me get over his death fast. I remember little about him. My mom gave me a photo of him carrying me on his shoulders when I was a kid. He was tall, with short dark brown hair and hazel eyes. He was one of those guys that could actually pull off a mustache without looking like a creep. You know the type, thick, dark, and well-trimmed. In the picture, he was laughing as I sat on his shoulders and pulled his hair in all directions. I don't remember the day the picture was taken, but I like looking at it.

"Aaron?" I turn around and see Zoë.

"Hey, what are you doing here?" I ask.

"Oh, you know," She grabbed a plate off the table and began to pile it high with food. "Had no food at my house and I figured your mom wouldn't mind." She flashes me a devilish grin; she knows my mom doesn't like her.

"Well, in that case, help yourself." I chuckle.

"I will," she says very matter-of-factly.

With her mountain of food ready, she plants herself next to me and begins to feast.

"Oh and, sorry about your cousin," She quips between mouthfuls of mac & cheese and casserole. "I remember him being pretty cool."

I nod in agreement. "Yeah, he was."

Zoë shovels more food into her mouth. Behind her I see my mother staring daggers at us. I shake my head at my mom, essentially telling her to leave it be. With a roll of the eyes, she walks into the living room.

"So?" Zoë urges.

"Huh?" I turn my attention back to her.

"I asked how Brian died?"

"Oh, um, I'm not exactly sure." I don't really want to think about Brian right now. Zoë sees my discomfort.

"Sorry, I didn't mean to pry, was just curious is all." She rubs her hand through her hair.

"No, it's ok, I just," I pause, not wanting to seem closed off. "I don't really want to know if I'm being honest."

She nods. "Yeah, I guess that's okay, sorry."

"Look, it's fine," I assure. "Although if I had to take a guess whatever it was, it had been going on for a while."

"Oh, what makes you say that?"

"Well, I saw his body at the wake. And what I saw was… a bit disturbing," I pause, taking a drink, in doing so I realize my hand is shaking. Zoë leans forwards, placing her hand on top of mine.

"Aaron, if you don't want to talk about it…" her voice full of concern.

I take a breath, remembering the scars on Brian's face and how much older he seemed. "He just looked so bad, like he aged twenty years."

"Aaron, your Aunt Jenny is leaving," My mom calls out.

"One second, Mom," I shout back. I look to Zoë as she removes her hand from mine. "Sorry about that."

Zoë is about to say something to me when she is interrupted by my impatient mom.

"Aaron, now!"

I frown, annoyed. Zoë laughs and stands up.

"I should probably get going anyways, now that I'm done with dinner," She says as she hands me her plate.

"Oh, why thank you madam," I mock. "Would you care for dessert?"

"No, thank you," Zoë plays along, "the meal was satisfactory. However, the service was awful. I'm afraid I will not be paying this time."

"When do you ever?" I say through a smile. Zoë leans forwards and gives me a hug. "Will I see you tomorrow?"

"I don't know. Wanna go to the aquarium?"

"Again?"

"What else we gonna do?" She laughs.

"I guess." I sigh. *She sure does love it there.*

"Aaron!" my mom shouts.

"I've got to go," I tell Zoë.

I start to walk away from her when she suddenly pulls me into a hug.

"I'm sorry about Brian," she speaks softly into my ear.

We part from our hug, and I stare into her eyes. I think about kissing her for a moment. But I don't, this isn't the time or place for that. I smile at her as she heads for the garage door. With a deep sigh, I walk into the living room and am confronted by the strange old lady that I now know to be my great aunt. She stonewalls me in the archway into the living room.

"Um, sorry," I apologize.

She doesn't respond. I'm not even sure she knows where she is, as her eyes are cloudy and her face expressionless.

"Um, okay," I start to squeeze past her. As soon as I do, she grabs me by my wrist and grips me tightly.

"Hey!" I shout and try to wrench my arm away from her to no avail. I look up at her to complain only to see her cloudy eyes have vanished, replaced with a look of sheer terror.

"You are in grave danger!" she croaks, her voice breaking with urgency.

"Aaron! Come say goodbye to everyone!" my mom shouts from the front door.

"You are next in line; he will come for you tonight," the old lady urges.

"What are you talking about?" I ask her, my voice rising in frustration.

"You are not safe!" she cries out.

My mom appears out of nowhere, stepping in between me and my supposed great aunt.

"Aaron, how many times do I need to call your name?" she demands.

She looks at me and my aunt who releases my arm. Her eyes have fogged over once again.

"Oh, hello Claudia," my mom greets, her voice full of contempt. "What are you two talking about?" she asks as she turns to look at me.

What do I say?

"Um, nothing, just saying hi," I can't stop looking at Aunt Claudia.

"Ok well, I think it's time for her to get going home now, don't you think Claudia?"

My aunt doesn't respond, I'm not even sure she could hear anything.

My mom takes my aunt's hand and guides her to the door, where another family member takes her. After that, the evening becomes a blur of goodbyes to family members and friends of Brian's. Finally, after everyone was gone, my mom turns to me.

"Honey, is everything ok?"

I nod my head, but I don't hear anything else she says. All I can hear is my aunts' final words: *You are not safe!*

Chapter 3

I find myself lying on the ground, staring up at the sky. The sky is black, devoid of any stars or moon. I sit up and try to make sense of my surroundings. I'm sitting in the middle of the street. There are tall, run-down buildings on either side of me, like downtown Chicago after the Bears lose a season. Panic starts to set in, my chest starts to tighten, and my breathing starts to rapidly increase.

How did I get here?

Nothing here seems familiar. Just a bunch of strange, boring looking buildings with a single street light. No cars, no people, just me and the city. Then it hits me, everything is dead quiet. Not a sound is heard, not even my own breathing. Panic sets in, and I get up off the ground, ready to run for help. As soon as I stand, I hear a loud roar, as though a bear is standing behind me. Without hesitation, I start running forwards into the night, away from whatever safety the streetlight offered me.

***

I run for what feels like forever. Finally, my energy gives out and I slow to a brisk walk.

What was that?

It didn't sound human, if anything, it sounded furious. Like a hunter that just lost its prey. Whatever it was, I pray I got away from it in time. I continue down the dark street and see another streetlight up ahead. As I approach, I see a large creature lying in the street in front of it.

A person?

I walk a little bit closer to the dark mass before a wave of terror comes over me. I feel my legs turn to jelly and the hairs all over my body stand on edge. The air is still, and the silence is almost deafening. My heart beats in my ears as I look at the creature before me.

What the hell is happening!?

"I'd run if I were you," a calm voice speaks into my right ear.

I shout and spin around, looking for whoever said that, only to realize that nobody is there. The street is still empty.

Hold on, this is not the street I came from.

My eyes go wide, and my knees start to shake as I look at the streetlight that should be behind me. Only now it's in front of me, along with the shapeless creature that laid before it. The creature begins to stand, and I am petrified with fear.

The first thing I notice about the creature is that it is wrapped in a dark cloak of some kind, and it is much bigger than I first thought. It stands on two legs and towers over the streetlight between us. Then I notice its hands, or should I say, lack thereof. Instead of hands, his forearms end in the upper torsos of two people, a woman on its left arm and a man on its right. Both are naked and gaunt, their skin stretched over their bodies like a rubber band that is about to snap. Their skin gleams white and their eyes are just open holes. Then I notice their mouths; they are hung open, screaming silently, endlessly. I want to run so bad, but my body won't let me.

Time seems to slow as I stare at the monster before me. I study the people it has for arms, feeling as though I recognize them. Then I see it, the vibrant red hair of the girl flows through the air as the monster breathes. The girl is Chloe!

Chloe? What the fuck is going on?

As I continue to stare at the increasingly massive monster in front of me, I hear the same voice from before angrily shout in my ear, "Run, you fool!"

The monster before me leans back and lets out the exact same screech I heard earlier. That is just what I needed to turn and propel myself away from the creature. As I run, I can hear the monster's heavy footsteps following me. I make the mistake of looking back only to see the monster's glowing yellow eyes stare back at me, into my very soul. I scream and keep running but feel like I am running on water. Then I realize… I'm not moving! Just running in place.

The monster screeches again and I look to my left to see Chloe staring at me. She is still silently screaming as she smashes right into me, sending me flying through the wall of a building. As I hit the ground, rubble from the wall showers over me. I gasp, struggling to breathe. I look up to see the monster leering over me. It goes to crush me with the male body it has for a hand, who also looks eerily familiar. I roll to avoid it and again, hear the monster roar in frustration.

I lift myself off the ground and start to run again, looking for any place to hide. The building I'm in seems to be a clothing store and I quickly take shelter from the beast behind a checkout counter. I press my back against the counter and quickly force my hands over my mouth and nose, trying to not make a sound. My left lung aches with every slight breath and I fear I might have broken ribs.

What the fuck is going on?

I listen and hear the monster tearing the store apart looking for me. I start to cry as I pray for help. Pathetic, as I never really did believe in God. Then again, I didn't believe in monsters either. The store goes silent, and I can only hear my labored breathing through my hands. I take the moment to slow my breath and remove my hands from my mouth.

The air falls silent. My body is so tense that I feel like stone. From off in the distance, I hear hooves galloping, followed by the cracking of a whip. I barely have time to make sense of what I am hearing before the counter I am cowering behind is suddenly ripped off the ground and thrown across the room. I spin around and fall on my back, looking up at the horrible creature, its face in full detail for me to witness. Its eyes are orbs of fiery yellow light in the middle of a black vortex of darkness. As I stare at its face, I see countless horrifying images flashing through my mind.

My mom, her chest ripped open, and her heart being feasted on by my nephew, Jake. My cousin Brian, his skin green from rot, crawling out of his grave, his teeth sinking into Zoë's neck. My sister, Chloe, naked and covered in blood, a malicious look on her face as she brings a sledge hammer down on my head, the headless corpse of a child beside me. All this and so much more. It's all too much for me to handle and I scream, covering my face in preparation for the monster to crush me into the floorboards.

"No! Get up, you coward!" the disembodied voice screams at me.

My reflexes kick in and I roll away from the monster as it brings its body down in force where I was laying. I feel an object appear in my hands. Looking down, I see an axe. I don't have time to think about it as I look at the beast and let out a scream of rage. Gripping the axe, I bring it down on the monster's head, splitting it in two.

The monster lets out a final, powerful screech and I am set flying backwards through the air by the force of his death howl. As I hit the wall, I feel my back crack and the building's ceiling begins to cave in on top of me. I claw at the air, trying desperately to stop it, but there is nothing I can do as the world around me collapses, burying me alive.

***

My eyes snap open to the ringing of the alarm on my phone. As air fills my lungs for what feels like the first time in my life, I take a moment to make sense of where I am. I'm lying in my bed, staring up at the ceiling. The light from outside sneaks into my room from behind my window shade. The whirring of the air conditioner unit faintly makes its way to my ears.

"It was just a dream," I laugh to myself.

Relieved, I begin to roll out of bed, but stop almost instantly as my whole-body screams in painful protest. The pain is so intense, I start to see black spots. I lay back on my bed and take notice of my chest. I suppress a scream as I see the entire left side of my body is black and blue, like I've just been hit by a truck.

"What the fuck?" I start to panic.

How did this happen to me?

As I stare down at my bruised body and try to make sense of what could've done this, I feel my neck and back start to strain and hurt. All over, I start to notice signs of my body having gone through serious trauma.

What happened to me?

My chest is one giant bruise, and I am struggling to breathe. Any attempt to move my body sends signals to my back which protests any movement with pain. I feel my feet and they ache as well, like I've just run a marathon. All over, my body is in misery. My bedroom door opens, and my mom appears in the doorway.

"Aaron honey, are you awake?"

I barely have the time or the strength to cover my body with my blanket. The sudden movement sends waves of pain all over my body and my vision goes dark.

I look over at her, "Yeah, Mom," I croak.

God, even my voice is a wreck.

"Oh, good. Listen I'm heading up to the store and I need to take your car. Your sister is out with Jake, and she took mine, so I hope you don't mind."

"Yeah, that's ok." I try to nod my head and grimace.

"Do you have anything going on today?" she asks, not noticing the pained look on my face.

"I don't know, maybe."

God, please leave!

"Ok, well just text me if you do go anywhere, ok?" She starts to close my door. "Love you!" The door closes and I'm alone again.

Thank God!

Now onto more important stuff, like figuring out what the absolute hell happened to me. What did I do yesterday? What could I have done that would leave me this wrecked without any memory of it? I feel my whole-body freeze in terror, the nightmare!

But no way, how?

That was just some stupid dream, all in my head. No way could any of that have happened. But if not that, then what? What happened to me? Did I do this to myself while I was asleep, or did someone do this to me? If not someone, something?

***

I couldn't let myself lay in bed all day. A normal person would've probably gone to the hospital. But given that I didn't know how I got hurt, let alone have the money to pay for the medical bills, I decided to toughen it out. No matter how much it hurt, I did have plans to hang out with Zoë today.

After lying in bed for half the day, I finally gathered the strength to roll out of my bed and stumble to my bathroom, where I gulped down a more than a concerning number of aspirin. After that, I took a freezing cold shower to help with the swelling all over my body and to wake me up. When I was done, I slowly make my way to Zoë's house, remembering my creepy aunt Claudia along the way.

"You are not safe!" Her warning echoes in my head.

Safe from what? A nightmare? Impossible. How could a nightmare hurt me? It's all just in my head, I must've run into something yesterday while playing with Jake. There's no way a dream could hurt me... right?

***

As I get to Zoë's front door, I could hear loud arguing coming from inside.

"But you let Brett take your car yesterday to his friend's house, how come I can't today?" Zoë shouts.

"Because when Brett takes my car, he pays for the gas. Also, he doesn't crash my car in the neighbor's yard!"

A man's voice, her fathers, retorts. "You're lucky you didn't lose your license then and there!"

"That was nearly two years ago!" Zoë shouts back.

"I don't care if it was fifty years ago. You are not taking my car and that is final!"

I sit on the ground as the commotion inside continues for another few minutes. Finally, all goes silent, and the front door opens, revealing Zoë. She looks beautiful as usual in a loose dark flannel jacket over a faded rock band t-shirt with her ratty black jeans and Doc Martens. The only thing that stands out from normal is her face, which is red with rage.

"Hello," I greet her, a dumb smile on my face.

"Fuck you."

"Oh, now, that's not fair, just cause you're a bad driver doe-"

"Not one more word!" She stops, pointing at me. Her face is contorted in anger. A normal person would shut up in an instant, but I know Zoë.

"Does this count?"

She stares me down for a few seconds before finally letting out an amused sigh.

"God, you are so annoying."

"Oh, you don't mean that," I chuckle, "In fact, I think you love me."

"Oh yeah, that's it," she laughs. "I love you with all my heart."

I sigh, "Well, looks like we're taking the bus."

Zoë frowns, "Why? Where's your car?"

"Mom took it. Chloe has the other," I explain. "So, we either walk or take the bus."

"Dammit," Zoë sighs, "bus it is."

We set out down the sidewalk towards the bus stop. As we walk, we talk about her dad and how much she hates him. She doesn't mean it; I know better than anyone what her dad means to her. But he is very strict and never forgets to remind you of your shortcomings. In Zoë's case, she is the ultimate fuck up, while her brother, Brett, is the golden child.

"I just don't get it. Brett steals from my dads' wallet and blows $500 on fucking lottery tickets. You'd think he'd be punished for it, right? Well, nope! Not dear old Brett. My dad just gives him another $20 because he remembered to clean the sink after he shaved. But I get into one accident and lose car privileges for life," Zoë vents.

"Yeah, well, it's not like you didn't crash it into the only tree in the neighborhood," I mock. "Or break into his shed and strip his lawn mower for scrap metal."

"Ok, first of all, it was a fucking accident. Second of all, the lawn mower thing was totally justified. We needed that stuff to make our robot ready for the robotics competition."

"Amazing the rare moments when you actually care about school."

"I just wanted Alan Moore's uptight ass to lose that fucking competition. Plus, don't act like you didn't get anything out of it."

"What did I get out of it, anyways? You took the prize money."

"No, my dad took the prize money. Besides, I taught you how to use a lockpick. That was pretty cool, right?"

"Oh yeah, such a useful skill. Not like I'll ever need that in my life," I say, laughing.

"It's a mystery why your mom doesn't want you hanging out with me. It's not like I'm a bad influence or anything."

"One that might never be explained." We chuckle some more.

"Does she know you're hanging out with me today?"

"Nah, she'd just complain about it."

"What if she tries to call you to see where you are?"

"Come on, you know me! My phone never has any service. The thing is so out of date I'm amazed every morning that it still turns on."

"Are you ever gonna get a new phone?"

"I don't know, unlike you I actually have to buy my phones, so I think I'll milk this piece of shit for all it got," Zoë says, as she smiles at me. I feel my heart flutter. We walk for a minute in silence, then Zoë speaks up.

"So… what were you trying to tell me yesterday?"

"Huh?" I ask, "Oh, you mean about Brian."

"Mhm," she nods.

I think for a moment. What was I going to say?

"You said he looked strange," she hints. "Like even for a dead guy."

"Oh, right," I say, as I imagine Brian's face flashing before my eyes.

"Aaron, you ok? You look like you've just seen a ghost."

"Yeah, sorry," I shake my head, my neck creaking painfully. "It's just, he looked so much older. Like he'd aged twenty years. And he had all these scars across his face."

"Scars?"

"Yeah, like he walked face first into razor wire," I explained. Now I couldn't get Brian's face out of my head.

We walked for a bit longer in silence, both of us thinking about Brian. Finally, it clicked for me.

Brian was the guy in my dream! The one that was the right arm for that monster. It was Brian, that's why he looked so familiar.

The realization sends shivers down my spine, which physically hurts, thanks to my injuries.

But what was he doing in my dream? And Chloe, too?

"Aaron, seriously are you ok? You look like you're about to pass out," Zoë urges. I realize I've stopped walking.

Why! Why are these dreams bothering me so much?

"Aaron!" Zoë shouts.

"Sorry, sorry," I say as I start to walk again. "I've just got a lot on my mind."

"If you need to talk-"

"No," I interrupt, "No, I'm fine. Just, let's talk about something else."

"Ok…"

After that, Zoë and I didn't say much to each other. We walk for a few more minutes to a bus stop. I find myself rubbing my side, the throbbing pain has gotten better, thanks to the aspirin, but it was still there. My body aches all over. But the pain seemed to fade when I looked at Zoë.

God, I'm hopeless.

We stood at the bus stop for a minute, the bus's tires screeching as it pulls up to us. Once we're on board, we continue to sit in silence. I guess that's one thing I really like about hanging out with her, we don't always need to be talking. Instead, we just keep each other company, both enjoying the world around us, Zoë especially.

She stares out the window, watching the city pass her by. She has always loved the city; she was made for it. Her punk aesthetic combined with her flawless looks and tough girl attitude made a city like Chicago her perfect little playground. We sit in silence the entire trip. After about a half hour the bus comes to a stop. The sky outside is ablaze as the sun begins to set. I look up at the driver as he shouts out, "Departures for Erie Street?"

"That's us!" Zoë jumps up,

"Wait, it is?" I ask, startled.

Oh no, not Erie St.

"Yep," Zoë said, and was out of the bus before I could ask anything else.

I chased after her, barely getting off the bus without my legs failing me. When I catch up to Zoë, I have to shout at her to get her attention.

"Hey, why are we here?"

She turns and looks at me, annoyed. "Oh, come on, you know why we're here."

Dammit, not Deacon.

"I thought you said we were going to the aquarium?" I complain.

"Yeah, I lied." She smirks. She doesn't look back at me.

"Oh, no," I say as I grab her by her arm, stopping her. "No, I told you I don't want anything to do with that douchebag."

"Come on, Aaron, again?" she says as she pulls her arm free. "Deacon isn't that bad,"

"Of course, he isn't, not to you, anyways. All he wants from you is to get in your pants," I say, with instant regret.

"Look!" Zoë raises her voice in anger. "I get you don't like him, but don't say shit like that, ok? He's my friend, too, and I'm not gonna listen to you bitch and moan about him. Ok?"

What is it with this guy?

I want to say that I don't want to go with her, and that Deacon is a creep. Literally anything to stop her from going. But I know that no matter what I say, it would just piss her off more. And I wasn't gonna let her go see him alone.

"Fine," I grunt. "Let's go see Deacon."

Chapter 4

I walk with Zoë in silence. She's clearly upset with me about what I said. Every part of me wants to turn around and walk home, but I know I can't. I don't trust Deacon alone with Zoë. I just don't know what she sees in him. He's arrogant, silver-tongued, and most concerningly, perverted.

We arrive outside of his bar, which is the most cliché shithole you could imagine in downtown Chicago. Rusty nails, torn-up leather seats, degenerate patrons, and a foul air that even rats gag on. As we enter, I take a quick look around and find the place to be mostly empty. A drunk man lays face down at the bar and a pair of burly biker-looking types are sitting in a booth. They give me and Zoë a curious look. We don't belong here, and they know it. Behind the bar, the bartender looks at us.

"Hey, Zoë, you here to see Deacon?"

Zoë nods her head, and the bartender presses a button underneath the counter. Zoë and I grab a seat in a booth and wait for Deacon to show up.

"Can you please tell me what we are doing here?" I beg Zoë. Her gaze is locked on the exit.

She turns to look at me. "He says he wanted to show me something cool. I figured you might like it, too."

I look up to see Deacon walking towards us. He's older than the two of us. I've never bothered figuring his age out, but I'd guess anywhere in his early twenties. He's tall and lean, with jet-black hair slicked back and some stubble on his face. He's wearing a nice leather jacket overtop a clean blue button-up shirt, with a pair of red tinted sunglasses hanging from his collar. Zoë sees him, too.

"Deacon, hey!" Zoë jumps up and gives him a big hug, one he eagerly returns.

After they part, he looks down at her outfit, more specifically her shirt. She is wearing a V-neck t-shirt underneath her usual flannel jacket. But it was obvious Deacon's mind was on other parts of her. He turns his head and looks at me coldly.

"So, you decided to come after all, huh?" His words are like the hiss of a snake in my ear.

"Yeah, I figured whatever it was that Zoë wanted here, she'd need a friend with her," I glare at Deacon.

"Well, that's kind of you, but I'm pretty sure little Zoë here doesn't need a chaperone, do ya?" He looks at Zoë, who seems annoyed.

"Can we cut the chest pounding already?" Zoë groans. "You said you wanted to show us something. So, what's up?"

Deacon smiles. "You're right; follow me, ladies."

As Deacon starts to walk towards the exit, I grab Zoë's arm and pull her face close.

"Zoë, seriously, I don't like this guy," I whisper.

She rolls her eyes. "Look, for the last time, Deacon is my friend. If you don't want to be here, fine. Go home. I don't care."

She rips her arm away from me and makes her way after Deacon. I want to throw a chair and storm off. But, of course, I don't and chase after them instead.

***

Zoë and I follow Deacon for what feels like forever. My legs, which are still sore from my dream, feel as though they are about to fall off. As we walk, Deacon talks all about his bar and his new car which he's getting fixed up in the shop. After that, he goes on and on about how one of these days Zoë needs to come out to his place.

"Bout time you see how a real man lives in this city," he sneers at me.

I bite my tongue, hoping that by not responding he'll grow bored or annoyed with me. After walking a bit further, Deacon stops just outside of a rather clean alleyway. He turns around and faces Zoë and I, a serious look on his face.

"Ok, now listen," he says, his voice calm. "Whatever you do, you cannot tell anyone about what I'm about to show you."

"Why, what are we about to see?" I ask.

"Just promise me. I could get in a lot of trouble if word of this place ever got out," Deacon looks straight at me.

"We promise," Zoë says. "Now for the love of God, will you tell us what we are doing out here?"

Deacon smiles and gestures to the alleyway to our right. "Just follow me this way."

We follow Deacon down the alley. The entire time, fear builds up in my throat. The tall dark buildings on either side of me remind me of my dream. As I remember the horror, I bump into Zoë, who has come to a stop before me.

"Sorry," I say to her.

She doesn't acknowledge me as Deacon stands before a smooth brick wall. He reaches his hands out and starts to feel the wall, caressing it gently. After a minute, he stops and smiles coyly. He puts some pressure on the wall and it cracks open, revealing a hidden entrance.

"Holy shit!" Zoë exclaims.

"Come on!" Deacon ushers us inside and closes the door behind us.

Once inside, we descend a flight of stairs. We go deeper and deeper until we finally find ourselves in an elegant waiting room. A soft yellow light emits from a chandelier above. The muted sound of music beats all around. In front of us stands a bouncer, who looks bored. He stares me and Zoë down, but Deacon simply walks towards him.

"Beautiful day, huh?" he says.

"Indeed," the bouncer nods, "could use some rain, though."

"To wash away the sins of man," Deacon answers.

The bouncer nods his head before looking back at me and Zoë. "They look a little young."

"No, they're 21. Got their ID's right here," Deacon hands the bouncer a couple of twenties.

"I dunno," the bouncer says, shaking his head, "these seem a little fake to me."

Deacon mumbles something under his breath, certainly nothing nice. He reaches into his wallet and pulls out a fifty, handing it over to the bouncer as well. The bouncer smiles and steps aside, allowing us to walk past him. Deacon looks back at Zoë and gives her a smile, flashing an annoyed look at me before facing forward.

He leads me and Zoë through a small hallway. The music around us grows louder. The hallway soon opens into a large club room. Tall pillars stand in the room, holding the ceiling up, I can only assume. The only light source is coming from large neon yellow lights on the sides.

Aside from the pillars, the room is large with a DJ booth in the center. Surrounding it is a large crowd of people, at least 200 people, easily. The room was massive yet tightly packed. The DJ played loud, aggressive music, and the people that surrounded the booth danced violently. I looked to Deacon to see him and Zoë laughing.

"Welcome to Purgatory!" Deacon shouts over the music.

Zoë smiles and looks at me, her eyes alight with joy. I smile back at her.

Ok, this place is pretty sweet.

I look around and notice a second story above us that contains a large balcony overlooking the dance floor.

"That's the bar!" he shouts at me, "who wants a drink?"

"Me!" Zoë laughs.

Deacon proceeds to lead us through the crowd. Overhead, lights start to shine down on the crowd, adding to the chaos of the room. I struggle to keep up with Deacon and Zoë.

"You're not safe," a gruff voice whispers in my ear.

I cry out with shock, spinning around to confront whoever said that. Only to see nothing but the dancing crowd. I turn back to find I've lost Deacon and Zoë. I start to push my way through the crowd in a panic.

I can't leave her alone with him!

As I make my way through the crowd, I see a large staircase leading up to the balcony. Already halfway up is Deacon and Zoë. Deacon looks down to see me, with a malicious grin. He puts an arm over Zoë and continues to lead her up the stairs. I go to start climbing the stairs when I am stopped by a large man in a pure black suit.

"Now where do you think you're going?" he asks, his hand gripping my shirt collar tightly.

"Upstairs, my friends are waiting for me." I point at Deacon and Zoë, but he doesn't look. Instead, he just chuckles.

"Kid, I don't know how you got in here to begin with, but upstairs is for VIP's only, and you sure as shit don't qualify."

"Wait, seriously, I'm with them up there!" I point to Deacon and Zoë. The guy doesn't even look in their direction.

"Yeah, bullshit kid." He grabs my arm and starts to drag me back through the crowd, "time for you to get going home."

I try to fight the guy, but I have no energy to fight. The painkillers are starting to wear off and any effort I make to break free from him sends waves of pain through my body. I drag my feet as I struggle against the guy, he puts up with it and continues to drag me away. Soon, I see the hallway where we entered Purgatory.

I can't leave Zoë alone with that asshole!

With all my strength I kick the guy dragging me in the legs, buckling them. As he tumbles to the ground, he drags me down with him. Once on the ground, the dancing crowd either doesn't notice us or doesn't care as they kick and stomp all over both of us. The music seems to grow louder.

My body screams in protest as I fight to stand back up. The guy who was dragging me grabs onto my legs, pulling me back down to the floor. Once he's on top of me, he screams something at me. But I can't hear what he's saying. I struggle against him, trying hard to get away from him, until finally he hits me in the side of the head, and my world goes dark.

***

I hear a little kid giggling, and my eyes snap open only to find myself standing in a room full of creepy as hell dolls. From what little I can see; I assume I'm in a workshop of some kind. Old dolls hang by strings from the ceiling. Even more are strewn about, littering the floor and tabletops. I am completely surrounded by them. The room is dark and musty smelling, the only source of light coming from a single candle, burning dimly in the center of the room.

As I make a step towards the candle, I hear the giggling again from right over my shoulder. I spin around only to see more dolls staring back at me. Their glassy, soulless eyes follow me, and I feel as though they can actually see me. I look back to the candle and notice a doll lying next to it.

Was that there before?

It is plain looking, with black wool hair and it is wearing a torn summer dress. But its eyes are black, and although I couldn't see much, I could feel its gaze burrowing into my face.

Oh, fucking hell!

I was dreaming again, that much was certain.

Please God don't let anything try and kill me!

"Oh, don't worry, I'll make it quick," a child's voice echoes around me.

Shivers run up my spine as I frantically look around the room for the source of the voice.

"What the hell do you want from me!" I scream, failing to mask my fear with anger. I hear more laughter, only this time it sounds sickly, almost gagging by its end.

Suddenly the dolls start to wriggle and writhe all around me. I look back to the candle to see the weird doll is now standing, its head tilted ever so slightly to the left, otherwise it was completely still. The dolls continued to rattle. Their strings began to snap from the effort.

"What do you think, silly boy?" The voice starts to warp into that of an old woman, filled with hatred. "I'm going to kill you!"

Suddenly, all the dolls come to life, throwing themselves at me. They begin to sink their tiny wooden teeth into my arms and legs, one even lunges for my face. I catch it in the air and use it to start beating the other dolls away, but with each one I send away, dozens more take their place. Soon, I'm buried in dolls. I start to scream, the stale air becoming scarce as the dolls continue to pile on top of me.

"They're just dolls!" A man's voice growls in my ear, in a thick Irish accent.

They're just dolls?

"Of course, they are!" the voice continues, "Quit making a fool outta yerself and get up!"

A calm comes over me and I stop struggling. Slowly, I start to get off the floor and the dolls fall to the ground all around me. They begin to scream with fury as I start to move forwards, ever so slowly as the dolls pool around me up to my chest. They continue to bite and scratch at me as I wade through them. Finally, I reach the weird doll that rests beside the candle. I grab it and with little effort, pop its head clean off. The dolls collectively shriek with pain, and they all fall to the floor, lifeless.

"What the fuck was that?" I ask aloud as I stare at the mass of dolls around me.

"That was disappointment," a gruff male voice booms, shaking the building violently.

"Who said that?" I shout.

"A bit brave of you," the building shakes again, "given that moments ago you were begging for mercy at the hands of dolls." The voice is loud but feels like it's whispering.

"What do you want?" I shout out, anger starting to burn away my fear.

"Silence!" the voice shouts, thundering around me like a cannon that had just been fired.

The building shakes around me once more, so violently that the walls and ceiling are blown away as though a tornado ripped the building apart. The dark room my eyes had grown used to was flooded by fiery orange light. I attempt to shield my eyes but to no avail.

As my vision adjusts, I see before me a tall, skinny man. He seems to be a living shadow, his body black as coal against the orange sky behind him. I can tell this man was trouble and fear starts to build up in my chest once again. A feeling I'm getting too used to, unfortunately.

Then I look to what he holds in his hands and true terror overwhelms me. In his right hand rests a long whip, made of what looks to be several human spines. The whip drips with blood, as though he had just pulled the spines out of a group of people moments ago. In his left hand, gripped tightly, was a human head.

I look up to meet the stranger's eyes only to find his head is nowhere to be seen. No! Not nowhere, but in his own hands! The head was bald, with pale white skin and a clenched jaw. Its gaunt eyes were shut, almost as though he was using all his strength to keep them closed. Even so, I could feel his gaze burning into me.

This guy seems familiar.

"That was very disappointing," the head spits. "I'll have to do better in the future."

"What do you mean? Are you behind these fucki-" I didn't have time to finish. The man cracks his whip at me with lightning speed. It hits me in the chest, sending me flying backward to the ground. My chest burns with fire as I struggle to catch my breath. I look down at myself to see blood flowing freely everywhere. Looking up, I see him strike his whip again.

"Run lad!" the Irish voice shouts in my ear.

I roll to my right, narrowly avoiding the next strike of the whip, but I'm given no more reprieve as the man continues to let fly at me. I continue to dodge as I scramble up and run away from him. As I run, I feel my heart pounding in my throat.

Why is this happening to me?

I continue running down the road of what looks like a medieval city. The brick road stretches before me and tall stone buildings tower on each side of me. The buildings grow taller and taller as the road becomes narrower. I run as fast as I possibly can. Behind me, I hear galloping and the cracking of a whip, followed by a horrid smell. I make the mistake of looking back.

The man now drives a horse drawn carriage. He cracks the whip at his horses, which are covered in rotting flesh with their bones showing through. I look forward and try to find an exit from the road I'm on, anything that could help me run from this psycho.

Is this the town from my nightmare?

I hear the crack of his whip once more followed by a searing pain in my right leg. I tumble to the ground. I try to force myself to stand up only to collapse under my own weight. The carriage behind me comes to a swift stop and the man lands in front of me.

Did he jump from his carriage?

The man looks down at me.

"Pathetic," he grunts, "to think you are the Son of David." With that, he raises his whip and brings it down on my face.

I attempt to roll out of the way, but my body has next to no energy left in it. All I manage to do is get my right cheek sliced open rather than the whole of my head.

Son of David? Then it clicks for me. *This is the guy that killed Brian!*

"Still fighting but failing." He clicks his tongue in disapproval.

I look up at the disembodied head with nothing but anger in my heart. "You. You killed Brian."

The head chuckles, and again goes to raise his whip. As he does, I feel my face sting, not from the gash in my cheek, but as though I'd just been slapped. The man seems to sense this as well.

"No! No, you die here!" he screams and brings the whip down at my face.

Time seems to slow and my vision clouds over, eventually leaving me in complete darkness. The raging scream of the headless man echoed endlessly in my ears…

Chapter 5

"Wake up you idiot!" a woman's voice commands. I feel a hard slap; my face stings and my ears ring out. I open my eyes slightly to see Zoë leaning over me, her stormy gray eyes full of fear.

"Oh, thank God!" she cries out, before slapping me again.

I groan in pain.

"That was for disappearing on us!" She looks down at me in shock. "And look at you! What the hell happened?"

I look down at myself and almost faint. I'm covered in blood and my chest burns as though I had fallen into a fire. My right leg is ripped open down to the bone. I can't handle what I'm seeing, my vision starts to go blurry, but Zoë slaps me again.

"No, stay awake!" She looks behind her, revealing Deacon talking on the phone.

"Did you call an ambulance?" she asks him. He nods at her and continues talking on the phone. Zoë turns back to me, "What the hell happened to you?"

I struggle to sit up but my body screams and black spots dance across my eyes. I look at Zoë. Her hair shines in the light of her phone, which illuminates the dark alleyway. I try to speak, but the words just don't form.

What do I say? How do I explain what's happening to me?

"Aaron?" She slaps me again. "What happened?"

I struggle to come up with a story. She would never believe me, even if she did, what could she do? I was losing my mind and, as it turns out, it was actually killing me. I wanted to cry and just break down in her arms. But I couldn't. What would she ever think of me? No matter what I'd say, it wouldn't matter, I couldn't speak. My throat was sore and dry, like I've never had a drink of water in my life.

Zoë's gaze doesn't leave me. The siren of an ambulance rings out in the distance, but her eyes stay on me. I want so badly to tell her that I was ok, to hold her hand and stroke her hair. Even on the verge of death, I can't stop thinking about how much I loved her. Deacon hangs up his phone and Zoë's attention snaps to him.

"Why didn't you tell me you'd lost him sooner?"

"I didn't notice he was gone! Sorry, it isn't my job to babysit him," he shouts at her.

"You brought us here! You should've been keeping an eye on us!" she shouts back.

Yeah, asshole.

The siren continues to get louder as Zoë and Deacon argue. Finally, she hangs her head in defeat. I know why she gives up, because she doesn't want to believe that he would intentionally let me get hurt. I want to say something, throw my hat into the ring of the argument, but I am barley awake, let alone strong enough to yell at him.

As we wait, I feel Zoë's hand intertwined with mine. I don't even have the strength to hold hers in return, but it seems I don't need to. Zoë's hand grips mine like a vice, warmth flowing up my arm from it. The ambulance arrives and as they fuss all over me, Zoë is pulled away from me. Once they have me stable, they put me on a gurney and load me into the ambulance. As they go to leave, Zoë stops them.

"Wait! Can't I come with him?"

"I'm sorry, miss, only family is allowed to accompany patients," the paramedic replies, closing the door on her. The last thing I see is Deacon standing beside her, and very calmly, putting his arm around her. He stares at me through the window, his eyes full of malice.

What an asshole.

***

I lay on a gurney as doctors and nurses push me into a room. A large, bright light floods my vision, and they start to cut my clothes away. One of the doctors says something about anesthesia.

"No!" I shout, terror filling every inch of my body. The doctors look at me with shock.

"Please, don't let me fall asleep," I beg, my voice cracking. "I'll be fine just, please."

With tears streaming down my face the doctors decide to start stitching me while I'm awake. They give me medicine to help with the pain, but I doubt it would've mattered if they didn't. My body was numb all over, pins and needles tickling my skin. I lay on the table, starring at the light above me trying my hardest to stay awake. After what feels like forever lying there, they finish. They wrap my wounds and send me to a hospital room.

***

As I lay in bed, I think about the man from my dream and everything that's happened in the past couple of days. Brian's death, my creepy aunt's warning, the nightmares, and even Deacon. It was all so much, and every second has felt like forever. My body is a mess of bruises and stitched wounds. I can barely move without passing out from exhaustion.

Don't fall asleep!

I'm miserable and have no idea what I'm supposed to do.

Why is this happening? How do I stop it? This all started after that first nightmare. The one where Brian died. Is that why this is happening to me? Am I going to die?

Someone must know something!

Aunt Claudia. Could she have something to do with it?

"Oh, thank God!" I hear my mother cry out.

I look to the door of my room to see my family. Mom rushes over to me. She goes to hug me but stops when she sees the bandages, her mouth agape. Chloe walks in carrying Jake.

"Aaron," Mom whispers, "what happened sweetie?"

"Mom…" I wheezed, tears already flowing. She finally hugs me, and I cry myself to sleep in her arms.

***

I jolt awake, so violently I almost fall out of the desk I'm sitting at. I look around to see I'm in an old classroom. The dim buzzing of the lights above me are the only sound I hear. The whiteboard in the front of the room is blank and there isn't another person anywhere to be found.

"God dammit!" I groan.

I struggle to get up from behind the desk, my bones creaking in effort and my fresh stitches threatening to come apart under the sudden movement. I start to make my way towards the door when a shrill voice speaks out from behind me.

"Mr. Ward, where do you think you're going?"

I spin around to see my teacher, Mr. Cray, standing at the whiteboard. He looks exactly the same as he did the last I saw him: tall and skinny, almost anorexic. His hair is gray and balding. Half-moon glasses rest on his fat nose and his large red skin blotch sits underneath his lips. I look around the room to see he isn't the only person to appear out of thin air. The room is filled with my usual classmates, all of whom are staring at me.

"Mr. Ward?" Mr. Cray speaks up, his voice high-pitched and nasally. "I asked where you were going?"

I feel anger stir inside me. *Why? Why the weird nightmares, the stupid gimmicks? Why not just kill me outright?*

"Mr. Ward, are you listening to me?" Mr. Cray shouts.

"Shut up!" I shout back at him, and his jaw drops in shock. "I don't get it! What is the point of this? Of trying to lull me into a sense of safety before trying to kill me!" My skin starts to burn, and my vision blurs.

"Aaron, I can assure you I have no idea what you are talking about," Mr. Cray reassures. "However I will forgi-"

"No!" I shout again. "No, enough with this bullshit!" I start towards the classroom door, forcing it open with all my strength. Stepping into the hallway, I begin to shout at the top of my lungs.

"Where are you, you shadowy prick?"

Silence fills the air. I sigh deeply and begin to walk down the hallway. I don't make it more than ten feet when I hear his voice.

"Oh, you certainly are brave," the man chuckles.

I turn around, only to find him directly in front of me. I have little time to react as he grabs me by my shirt and lifts me into the air with one hand. He raises his severed head in his other, bringing it up to my eye level. The head's eyes remain closed, yet I feel his gaze bore into mine.

"What do you want with me?" I scream at the head, my voice breaking.

The head only chuckles.

"Why is this happening to me?" I'm starting to cry again.

I just want answers.

"Dullahan," the head says.

"What?"

"Dullahan," he repeats, "That's what I am. Or more specifically WHO I am."

"Why are you trying to kill me?" I feel an eerie calm overtake me.

"Because that is the price that must be paid," he sighs. His face relaxes and I can see he's clearly exhausted.

"What price?" I beg.

He doesn't answer me. Instead, he opens his eyes. Or at least, starts to. Time seems to slow as they open. A sliver of pure white light peaks through his eyelids and my blood runs cold.

I feel a pull from the center of my back, and I go flying through the air. I smash into a brick wall and my back feels like it's about to snap in half as the wind is knocked out of me. As I slump to the floor, the Dullahan's whip wraps itself around my leg, cutting into the flesh deeply. I scream in agony as he pulls me back towards him.

"I will not let you interfere!" the Dullahan shouts as he pulls me towards him.

I have no idea who he is speaking to.

His whip digs deeper into my leg, and I fear it will cut it off. Once the Dullahan has me in front of him, he rests his foot on my chest and begins to press down with all his might. I feel my lungs squeeze, the air within being forced out. The school hallway starts to crumble around me as my vision grows dark.

"You aren't escaping that easily," he hisses

The walls of the building fall away as the roof is ripped away. Then I feel the floor beneath me start to break. Just when I'm about to give up, just as what little energy I had left was about to leave my body and my eyes closed forever, the floor gives way to a deep and dark canyon below. As I fall, I watch the Dullahan swing his whip at me, roaring with rage as he tries to catch me. He misses, and I continue to fall.

***

I fall for what feels like hours when I begin to smell damp, rotten air and feel the temperature begin to rise. Then I hit water. My body stings all over as I belly flop into its warm and foul-smelling depths. As I sink, I see a bubble of air below me, rising to meet me. The air envelopes me and I begin sucking in greedily, musty though it may be.

The pocket of air carries me upwards, until finally I break the surface of the water and find myself in the middle of a dark swamp. Trees as big as skyscrapers surround me and I hear flies buzzing and birds cawing. I look to my right to see a large swath of dry land and I begin to make my way to it. Once out of the water, I look around.

Where am I now?

"Well, a swamp you daft shit."

I turn to see a man standing behind me. He's short and buff, with long brown hair and a thick red beard. His eyes are piercing blue, and a large scar stretches across his left cheek.

"You know, I'm so sick of people just appearing out of nowhere behind me," I say.

"Sorry 'bout that." Suddenly he's to my right. "But it's your fault." Now he's standing to my left.

"Look, stop!" I shout at him. "Stop the charades, just fucking kill me, please, if that's what you really want."

"Kill ye?" He howls with laughter. "Laddie, if I wanted ye dead I'd have just shoved yer head back under the water when ye came up for air!" His voice is deep and warm, with a thick Irish accent.

"Then what do you want with me?!" I shout at him.

"Shhhhh!" He cups his hand over my mouth, looking around in search of something. He looks me in the eyes and whispers, "You shouldn't be so loud, boy, that's how he finds ya."

I move his hand away from me, "Who, the Dullahan?" I ask.

"Yes. That cunt 'ill find ye and kill ye just as fast the more trampling and screaming ya do around here."

"Look, I have no idea what's going on, so can you stop being so fucking vague before I try to kill you myself?"

He holds his hands up in a gesture of peace. "Ok, you're right. Let's talk." He sits down on a fallen tree and gestures for me to do the same. Once I've sat down, he introduces himself as Finnan.

"Ok, Finnan, what the fuck is happening to me?" I ask him.

"Well, I'm pretty sure that Dullahan bastard is trying to kill ya."

I shake my head in frustration. "Of fucking course he is! But why is he trying to kill me?"

"Well, to be honest, I don't know. All I do know is that he's been killing our family line for centuries. And it don't look like he's stopping anytime soon." He says all this in a very matter-of-fact tone.

"Wait, are you dead?"

"Well, good lord, lad, what did you think I was?" He chuckles.

I pause for a moment in disbelief. "Am I dead?"

"Not yet!" Finnan chuckles some more.

"Ok well, how is it you're here then?"

"Again, I don't know. I don't know much of anythin'. Except for the fact that Dullahan bastard is trying to kill you, like he does to everyone he sees."

"So do you know why?"

"Like I said, I think it has something to do with yer bloodline. See, me and you," he points to me then himself, "are related. Technically speaking I'm your great, great, et cetera, et cetera uncle," he chuckles to himself.

"Ok, that still doesn't answer my question."

"Lord boy, you sure are impatient, aren't cha?" Finnan replies. "My guessin' is the Dullahan is a curse of some kind who is tryin' to kill all the members of our family. Well, the men, that is."

"That does nothing but give me more questions." I rub my eyes. "Is there anything helpful you can tell me? Like, why are you only now showing up? Or how is it that nothing is trying to kill me right now?"

"Oh, that's easy. So, to what I gathered about this place, this dream we're in mind ya, it isn't the Dullahan's to control."

"Bullshit, I've seen him rip buildings apart and appear out of nowhere just like you. Also, he keeps sending those creepy as hell nightmares my way."

"Exactly!" He claps me on the shoulder. "Listen lad, the Dullahan is very powerful, yes. And he can manipulate parts of this world we are in, but that doesn't mean he controls it." Finnan starts to look around, his head on a constant swivel. "You do."

"What do you mean I do.?" I laugh, "I haven't been able to do anything in this place except get my ass kicked!"

"Then explain ya leg." Finnan points to my leg. I look at it to see that it's completely fine.

"What about it?"

"Didn't the Dullahan wrap you up in that whip of his? Almost ripped the damn thing off if I saw correctly."

With his words, I feel the familiar searing pain I felt earlier. I look down to see my leg has started to bleed.

"Ah, there ye go!" Finnan replies.

Blood is flowing freely from my leg and the pain begins to fade away into numbness as my leg seemingly begins to fall off. I start to panic, until Finnan leans over and smacks me. I look at him and am about to scream when he interrupts.

"Stop doin' that to yerself!" he snaps, "it's all in your head. As long as you don't let it, nothing the Dullahan or anything he sends after ya will be able to hurt ya, well, for long, at least."

I look back down to my leg to see the blood flow is slowing and note that the feeling is returning.

"See, just concentrate. Imagine the wound closing up and the blood fading away."

As he speaks, my leg begins to return to normal, as though nothing ever happened to it. I start to laugh loudly.

"No!" Finnan shushes me, "Not too loud now. I can tell, he's close."

"What?" My heart skips a beat.

"Like I said, he doesn't control things around here, but that doesn't mean ya safe from him, he can still hurt ya. Every second you spend asleep, he hunts for ya, sending out nightmares to trap and hurt ya, even try to kill ya, until he arrives."

I hear far out in the distance the cracking of a whip.

"Moreover, just because you can do that shite with your leg don't mean you'll be able to do much against him. He is unstoppable."

"There has to be some way to stop him?"

Finnan shakes his head. "Many have tried over the centuries. Ya father, grandfather, uncle, that cousin of yours. Everyone ye've ever known and hundreds more have tried to stop him, tried to fight him. In the end, they all died."

My heart sinks. "Then what's the point? Why try when it's inevitable?"

Finnan stares at me, his eyes heavy with sorrow.

"Answer me! What's the point if nothing I do can stop him? Why shouldn't I just let him kill me?"

Finnan continues to stare at me. Finally, with a deep sigh, he stands up. As he does, he slowly begins to shapeshift. He starts to become taller, and leaner. His beard recedes into his face, leaving behind a brown mustache. His hair becomes shorter, and his eyes grow softer and darker.

Before I knew it, I was no longer staring at Finnan, but my dad. I have no words; my mouth hangs open in shock. Again, the sound of a whip echoes from far away.

"Hey kiddo," he smiles softly. I stand up, shocked.

"Dad?" My voice a whisper as the word is caught in my throat.

He goes to speak when I throw myself at him, hugging him tightly. In the distance, I hear horses galloping and a whip snapping, growing louder by the second. My dad pushes me away.

"Aaron, son, listen to me," he grasps my shoulders, "we don't have much more time before the Dullahan finds you. So, I need you to make me a promise."

"What?" I ask as the sounds of hooves hitting the water echo around me. The cracking of a whip and the smell of blood and rotten flesh fill the air.

"Promise me that no matter what happens to you, no matter how hopeless it seems…" a horse's neigh tears through the air followed by the grunts of the Dullahan, "…that you will never stop fighting to stay alive. Because if you die, Jake will be next!"

From behind my dad, the Dullahan's carriage explodes out of the thick swamp brush and starts to make its way towards us. Following behind him is a trio of tornados, tearing apart the swamp.

"Aaron Ward!" the Dullahan shouts out, his whip cracking through the air. "There is no running from me!"

I have no time to react as my dad pushes me into the water. The last thing I see of him is the Dullahan's whip ripping through the air. Its tip aimed for his face.

Chapter 6

I wake screaming for my dad. My mom, who is sleeping in the chair beside my bed, jumps awake and rushes to hold me. She sits on the bed, cradling me softly as I cry into her arms. She runs her fingers through my hair and eventually I calm down. We sit like that for a while, my sobs fading along with my tears. Eventually, my mom falls asleep beside me, thinking I must have as well.

I lay beside her, the eerie quiet of the room broken only by my mom's light snoring. As I stare up at the dark ceiling of my hospital room, I think of what my dad said to me, "…if you die, Jake will be the next!"

Does that mean Jake will start to have these nightmares as well?

If that's true, I have no choice but to find a way to stop this. But how? So far, the only person who seems to know what's happening to me is Finnan. Even so, he doesn't know much more than me.

My Great Aunt! Maybe she knows how to stop it. But how do I find her?

I look at my mom, she seems so tired even as she sleeps. Her eyes are dark, with deep bags underneath. I assume it's stress. First my dad dies, then Chloe has a baby in high school, now I'm in the hospital. I feel bad for her, her life has never been easy.

I can't die.

That would crush her. And it would get Jake killed as well. If that happens, what then? Does the Dullahan go on to other victims? Or will he remain forever, killing everyone in the family right out the gate? No matter what the outcome is, I can't let him win. I must survive.

***

I struggled to stay awake over the next few days. Doctors regularly tried to give me medicine to help me sleep, and my mom wasn't too happy with me staying awake either. I couldn't tell them why; they simply wouldn't understand. Who would? If I tried, I know they'd just give me a bunch of pills and call me crazy. I couldn't allow that. I needed to stop what's happening to me, and I couldn't do that from a padded room.

I felt stronger as each day went by and was soon ready to leave the hospital. Eventually, I came up with the lie that I had gotten jumped by a group of dudes in the alley after failing to sneak into a club. The doctors were a little skeptical, but it was enough to warrant my injuries and calm my mom down. Chloe and Jake came by to visit every day, and my mom never left the room unless she had to.

Zoë didn't come by at all. I started to worry, until the day came when I was ready to be discharged. The doctors and my mom were all very against me leaving so soon, but I knew there wasn't enough time for me to make a full recovery. I was able to stand unassisted, although barely, and after enough arguing, my mom finally caved into letting me go home.

As I was being wheeled out by the doctors, I saw Zoë waiting for me by the exit. She smiled at me and as I struggled to get out of the wheelchair, then she pulled me into a hug.

"Thank God you're okay." She pushes me away, holding me by my shoulders. She stares into my eyes, "Don't you ever do that shit again!" I start to laugh, and she slaps me.

"Ow!" I yelp, "what was that for?"

"I'm being serious," her stormy-gray eyes bore into me, "you really scared me."

"I'm sorry. I just," I pause, uncertain what I should say.

"Just, please tell me you're okay? That you'll be taking it easy from now on?"

"I promise."

She smiles at me, and I can't tear myself away from her eyes.

"I was worried about you. You really scared me."

"I'm sorry. It wouldn't have happened if we hadn't gone to that stupid club."

"Now that's not fair. Deacon was trying to show us a fun time," Zoë argues. "It was fun, until…"

"Until you realized I was missing," I replied. "Deacon saw me, he saw me getting separated from you. Then he watched as the bouncer dragged me away from the bar."

"Aaron, Deacon didn't see anything! The second we both realized you were gone we started looking for you." She pauses for a second, as though choosing her words carefully. "He was worried about you."

I scoff at her. "Bullshit. Zoë, he saw me! Didn't even blink as that bouncer dragged me away!"

"You must've been seeing something else. Aaron, I promise you, he wouldn't do that!"

"To you maybe."

"Look, I get you don't like him. But would I trust him for a second if I thought he was capable of hurting me or you?" Stress was beginning to strain her voice.

I stare at her, my blood beginning to boil. "Are you serious? Of course, you would, you're only in love with the douchebag!"

She slaps me, harder than before. Spots begin to dance in my eyes.

"You have no right to talk about him like that. I know you don't see it, but he is a good guy." She's starting to tear up, "and so, what if I like him, it's not like that's any of your business!"

"Of course, it is!" I shout at her.

"Oh why? Because you think you love me, too?" she shouts back.

We both go quiet.

She knows?

"You're in love with me, right?"

She already knows the answer. I just stare at her, unsure of what to say.

"Just say it already."

"Yes," I mutter.

"And because you *think* you love me, that gives you the right to push Deacon away from me."

I continue to stare at her, my eyes burn, and I realize I wasn't blinking. She knew I liked her and never thought to say anything?

"Right?"

"You knew I loved you and never said anything?" I whisper, my eyes watery.

She scoffs at me. "What was I supposed to say? 'Sorry Aaron, I know you're in love with me, but I don't feel the same way, can we still be friends?'"

My mom's car pulls up beside us. I hang my head, defeated. I wanted to yell at Zoë, pour my heart out to her, make her see how bad she just hurt me.

"Well? Aren't you gonna say anything," she begs.

There is nothing to say.

Heart-broken, I turn and head for my mom's car.

"Say something!" Zoë demands.

I get into the car and slam the door behind me. Without saying anything, my mom drives away.

***

I sip away at an energy drink. I feel exhausted; just the effort of raising the drink to my lips feels like rolling a boulder up a hill. My mom still doesn't say anything to me; her mother's intuition must tell her enough not to. As we drive, I finish my drink, then look at my mom, "I want to go see Aunt Claudia."

"What?"

"I want to go see Aunt Claudia," I repeat. "I need to see her."

"No, I'm not taking you to see her."

"Why not?" I look at her, confused.

"Because you're still in bad shape. You need to go home and get some rest. Relax for a few weeks." She explains.

"Mom, I get it. You're just trying to protect me. But I'm fine."

"No, you are not!" she raises her voice, "Aaron you just spent a week in the hospital. You're covered in stiches and bandages; you haven't slept in days. You're in no condition to be going to another state to visit some crazy woman!"

"But-"

"But nothing," she cuts me off. "I will not let that woman put crazy ideas about demons into your head!"

Demons? Does my mom know what's happening to me?

My mom goes silent as we pull into our driveway. We're barely in park before she is out of the car. I sit in disbelief for a moment before following her. As I step through the doorway I'm surprised by Jake, who jumps out from around a corner and screams playfully.

"Uncle Aaron!" He runs to hug me, painfully throwing his weight onto my bad leg. I stumble backwards, catching myself on the door frame.

"Jake, no!" Chloe shouts at him.

He lets go of me and turns to face her.

"Uncle Aaron is still hurt, okay? He can't be rough housing right now."

"But... I'm bored," he says.

Chloe looks at me and smiles apologetically. "Okay then goofball, let's go to the park, huh. Maybe some of the neighborhood kids are there playing kickball."

"I hate kickball."

"Jake, let's leave Uncle Aaron alone, please." Chloe raises her voice, something that I hardly ever hear her do.

Jake immediately gives up and starts to put his shoes on.

"Thanks, Chloe," I say.

"Of course," she looks me up and down, "How are you feeling?

"I've been better, but fine now that I'm home." I try to reassure her.

"Mhm." She clearly isn't convinced. "So, what happened to you again?"

"Got jumped and a few guys started beating the crap out of me." I lie.

"And what exactly were you doing in an alley?" she asks.

"Um, just waiting for Zoë."

Dammit, she sees right through me.

"In an alley?" she says, clarifying.

"Look, it doesn't matter why I was there. Point is. I was and that's what happened."

"Aaron," Chloe sighs, "whatever is going on with you, that's your business. I'm not gonna lie, I don't believe you for a second with that who 'I got jumped' story. If you won't tell me or mom the truth, that's on you. But know that we're both very worried about you right now."

"You don't have to be." I try once more to assure her, "I'm fine. Everything is fine."

"Whatever, Aaron." She shakes her head in disappointment.

Jake comes running back with his shoes on. Chloe takes him by the hand and starts to head out the door. Before she closes it behind her, she looks back at me. "Try not to get yourself killed doing whatever it is you've been doing." With that, she slams the door behind her.

I stand there for a moment, taking in the whole conversation. *I know she's worried about me, but there's nothing she can do to help me. And she certainly wouldn't believe me fI told her what was happening to me.*

With a deep breath, I make my way to my mom's bedroom. By the time I reach the door, my leg is already starting to burn. I open the door to reveal my mom sitting on her bed, holding a picture frame. I step into the room and make my way to her bed, flopping down on my back with a sigh of relief.

We stay like that for a moment, taking in the peace and quiet before finally I sit up. It's then I notice the picture she's holding. It's one of my dad and Chloe when she was just a kid. He looks the same as he did in my dream.

Will I ever see him again?

My mom puts the photo on her lap and turns to me.

"Aaron, do you know how your father died?" she asks.

I shake my head. I've never cared to find out. He was dead, that was depressing enough. Although now, with everything that's been happening, I think I know the answer.

My mom takes a deep, shaky breath. "He died in his sleep one night, for no reason at all." She pauses and wipes away a tear from her eye. "When the doctors tried to find out why he died, they said at first that there was nothing wrong with him. But you want to know what they found?"

I nod my head.

"He was covered in scars." She wipes away a fresh tear. "They were recent they said. And they said," she takes a deep breath, "they said it looked like he'd been whipped."

"So, he was hurt?" I feigned ignorance. I needed her to tell me everything she knew.

"By something. From what they said it looked like he had been whipped, repeatedly." She takes another deep breath. "But that wasn't all. Eventually, they found what killed him." She wipes more tears from her eyes.

"Mom, it's ok if you need a minute." I want to hug her, but I know that she'll just break down if I do, and I need her to finish telling me everything.

She smiles at me and after a moment speaks again, "They found water in his lungs."

"Water?"

"According to the doctors, yes. They said he drowned."

What a horrible way to go.

"Mom, do you have any idea what really happened to him?" I ask calmly.

"No, no, and I don't want to." She starts to get up, but I grab her arm.

"Mom, if you have any idea what happened to dad, I deserve to know." I let go of her arm. "It might be important."

"No, no, this was a mistake. I shouldn't have-"

"Shouldn't have what?" I cut her off. "Shouldn't have told me how my dad died? And that he died under mysterious, no, impossible, circumstances? Mom, you know there's something more to this, and I need to know the truth."

My mom stands there for a moment, as if deciding whether or not to talk to me or run away from me. Finally, she starts talking again.

"He started having horrible nightmares. Not long after your uncle died. He'd wake up in the middle of the night screaming. And the blood-," her voice breaks, and she takes a moment before she continues, "he was almost always hurt whenever he woke. I thought he was just hurting himself in his sleep, but he swore he wasn't. He would rant about some demon. After a while he just stopped sleeping. He became paranoid, almost crazy."

"When he died, did he say anything? Anything about what was happening to him.?" I ask desperately.

"No, no nothing. He just…" She wipes her nose, tears welling in her eyes. "He just talked about you. That day, he did nothing but watch you. He held you and played with you." She grabs the picture frame with him and Chloe in it, "and before he went to sleep, he said how much he loved you and your sister."

Sadness hits me as a chill passes through my chest.

He knew he was going to die that night.

"Mom, we both know what happened to me wasn't because I got mugged in that alley," I say as she sniffs and wipes the tears away from her eyes for the last time. "If what is happening to me is the same as what was happening to Dad, I need to know everything I can."

"Aaron, what you're saying can't be real."

"Mom, look at me." When she does, I lift my shirt up, revealing the bandages over my chest. "This was caused by a whip. The same one that hurt Dad."

"Aaron, that is nonsense."

"I know. I know it's crazy, Mom. But it's the truth." I stand up and look her in the eye, "That's why I need to see Aunt Claudia. She told me that this would happen to me, back after the funeral. I need to talk to her."

My mom, with a defeated expression on her face, finally tells me where I can find my great aunt. She gives me some money, enough for gas and food. Before I go, she begs me to be careful.

"I promise. No matter what I'm going to find out why this is happening to me. And I'll stop it." And with that, I go to leave, taking one last look at my mom before I walk away from her for what I hope isn't the last time.

***

According to my mom, Aunt Claudia lived in the Upper Peninsula of Michigan, in a town called Gladstone. I knew that energy drinks and coffee wouldn't be enough to keep me awake for that long of a drive, and then for however long of a conversation with my aunt. So, I decided, ruefully, to get some sleep.

Before I could though, I needed to take a shower. I strip off the clothes my mom had brought me and let them fall to the floor. I start to make my way towards the shower, but I stop. Turning instead to the mirror above the sink, I see my reflection and I'm a shadow of who I was. My hair, normally short, is grown out and sticks up in all directions. My skin is pale, almost gray. I have puffy, dark bags under bloodshot eyes. I'm thin, as though all my muscle had faded away with my tan.

I can't believe how different I look; it's only been a couple weeks since school ended. I can't even move my body, out of shock or even fear. Then anger begins to bubble up inside of me slowly. I ball my fists up and I feel an overwhelming urge to shatter the mirror. I stop myself, forcing my hands to relax.

I step into the shower and the hot water flows over me. My chest begins to sting lightly as the water reaches my stitches. I stand there for what feels like hours, basking in the warmth. Finally, I finish my shower. As I step out, I feel my bad leg buckles under my weight. I lean forward to catch myself on the sink but miss. I land on the ground hard and lay there, frustrated with myself.

After picking myself up off the floor, I make my way into my bedroom. I don't even bother to dress myself as I fall into bed, wrapping the blanket around myself. I stare up at the ceiling, bracing myself for what's about to come once I close my eyes…

Chapter 7

I stare up at the ceiling of my bedroom. I look around, confused. I was exhausted just moments ago, and now I can't fall asleep. Why is that? I sit up, feeling the stitches across my chest stretching in the effort. I look to my window and see the sky outside slowly begins to darken as the sun begins to set. I stand up and stretch. My chest stings and I start to pull my clothes on. As I make my way towards the door I realize:

It's so quiet.

I turn the handle and open the door, stepping out into my hallway. I wander about the house for a minute, looking for my sister or mom. I listen for Jake, only to be met by deafening silence. I make my way back towards my room, determined to get some sleep. I step back into my bedroom and close the door behind me.

The silence grows louder all around me as I stand at the foot of my bed. The beating of my heart begins to intensify, growing louder with each passing second. I reach for my phone and start to call my sister, but the call gets no signal. The flow of blood in my ears accompanied with the furious beating of my heart starts to sound like waves roaring in a storm. I throw my phone down on my bed, frustrated.

Why is it so quiet?

I make my way back towards the window, hoping for some fresh air. I stick my head outside and breathe deeply. The silence follows me. I pull my head back into my bedroom and step back into the center of the room.

From behind me, someone knocks on my bedroom door. I open my mouth, about to tell whoever it is that they can come in but stop myself. A sharp pain hits my chest and fills me with fear. Slowly, I make my way towards the door, my heart pounding in my ears. My hand reaches for the door knob, and rests shakily on it.

I'm so sick of being scared!

Rage fills me and I pull the door open, forcing myself through the doorway. Only it isn't the hallway of my house I step into, but instead I find myself in a padded room, like that of an insane asylum. The air smells rancid and stale, and the floor is filthy, covered in old stains of what looks to be puke, urine, and blood. I turn around to leave and find my bedroom door is gone, replaced with more padded wall. I spin in circles, hoping to find a door to run to, only to be disappointed.

My heart is beating faster than ever before, and the silence continues to grow louder. I start feeling the walls, hitting them in the hopes that they would fall away. They don't give. An old LED panel on the ceiling emits a dull, yellow light. The buzzing fills the room. My ears, once desperate for sound, bleed as the monotone hum echoes all around me. My vision blurs, and I struggle to breathe. Hyperventilating, I fall to the ground, panic overtaking me.

Time seems to stretch on forever. I lay on the floor of the padded room and start to wonder how long I've been here. Minutes? Hours? Days? I fear I'm going crazy as the thoughts tear through my mind. Then, I remember what Finnan said to me:

"…just concentrate. Imagine the wound closing up and the blood fading away."

I was able to heal my leg last time! If I could do that, what's to say I can't make a door for me to escape from here?

My heart rate begins to slow as I work to catch my breath. My vision clears up. I focus on a long crack in the padding, one that looks like it could be for a false door.

And so, it shall be.

I push myself up off the floor and press the palm of my hand on the wall; willing it to open. At first, nothing happens.

Of course, it can't be that easy.

Again, I try, and nothing happens. I start to pound on the door. With each punch I feel the solid wall behind the padding refusing to give. Fury fills me as I hit the wall repeatedly for what feels like hours. Eventually I grow tired, and I fall to my knees, my bruised hand resting against the wall. My anger giving way once more to despair as my eyes begin to tear up.

"…if you die, Jake will be the next in line!" My dad's voice rips through the air. Rage fills me once more, lifting me off the floor. I stare at the crack in the padding and focus intently.

"You're a fucking door," I grunt, and with all my strength throw myself against the wall.

***

The first thing I notice is the cold, chilling me to the bone as I pick myself up off the floor. I quickly look around to make sure the room I'm in isn't another padded cell. Instead, I start to wish it was. All around me are small, cubic lockers built into the walls. The doors are white, with the paint peeling off them revealing the black, cold metal beneath. The room itself is narrow yet long, almost a hallway. At the other end of the room is a set of big, hospital doors.

"A morgue?" I whisper, my voice echoing off the lockers, growing louder as it slowly turns my whisper into a yell.

I walk down the hallway. With each step, I feel as though I'm walking waist deep through mud. My legs struggle to move, and it isn't long before I'm too tired to do it anymore. My bad leg is throbbing with pain.

As the echo of my voice finally fades away, the lockers closest to me rumble. All along the room, the lockers begin to shake violently in unison. I know whatever is about to happen will end badly for me. I try to run but can barely lift my feet off the ground. Suddenly the locker closest to me opens, and from it exits a table with a body bag lying on top of it.

My body freezes as I stare at the table before me. I look on to see all the other lockers stop shaking. A few more open, and tables with body bags fly out from them. This goes on for a few moments and soon the lockers stop opening. Before me lies dozens of body bags, maybe hundreds.

The one closest to my right begins to move. It shuffles slowly, and I start to hear the zipper of the bag rattle. The temperature of the room drops even further, and my hands start to tremble, as the bag unzips. Once it's finished, the room falls silent as nothing moves or makes a sound. Then, ever so slowly, a person rises from the bag.

It's a man. His hair is dark and receding. His skin is pale and sickly, and his face is gaunt and lifeless. His eyes are closed, his head limp as his face looks to the ceiling. More of the bags that lie before me begin to unzip themselves, each revealing one person after another. Like the man before them, they all look long dead. The air, once stale, is now rank, with the smell of rotting corpses.

I realize I'm shivering and force my body to be still. To my left I see another man. He is younger, around my age, with a sharp jawline, shaggy, dirty blond hair, and light stubble on his chin.

Brian?

I take a sharp breath and the, now foul, air forces me to cough. The head of every corpse snaps aggressively in my direction. The eyes of the man who looks like Brain snap open. Dull and yellow eyes with large pupils glare at me, hungrily. With a shrill shriek, he launches himself at me. The other corpses follow his lead.

I scream with rage as I knock Brian away. As he falls to the ground, more corpses climb over him and lunge at me. I run away as adrenaline propels my body forward, ignoring whatever was making it so difficult to walk earlier. I run back to where I came from, batting away the corpses as they chase and dive after me.

All around me now, I hear the cracking of a whip and the thunderous galloping of horses over the shrill screams of the dead. The horde of undead chase after me, constantly at my heels as I kick and punch them away. More and more lockers open as I run past them, and corpses pour out from them, adding to the wave of death behind me. A locker opens in front of me, and the body of an old woman launches herself out at me. I dodge and dive onto her table, forcing myself into the locker from whence she came.

Once I'm inside the locker, the stench of rotting flesh grows tenfold. The enraged sounds of the undead boom all around me as they pound their fists against the door. The space I lay in is small and dark. I feel around, hoping to find something that could save me.

God, why can't I force myself awake?

Suddenly, over the screeching and pounding of the corpses, I hear a horse's neigh followed swiftly by the cracking of a whip.

"Aaron Ward!" The Dullahan's voice thunders, shaking the locker I'm hiding in. "Come out from there and I'll let your death be a quick one!"

I continue to feel around my locker, finding nothing of use.

Think dumbass, think!

"Nothing in there can help you, Aaron," the Dullahan roars. "Come out here now and make this easy for the both of us!"

"I'm not afraid of you!" I shout.

The Dullahan chuckles, "Oh, but you will be…"

The locker I hide in shakes violently as a large, mangled dent appears in the steel. The loud snap of a whip follows, tearing through the air and sending shivers through my spine.

Think dammit!

Another blow strikes the door, and the locker shakes and groans.

"There is nowhere to run, nowhere you can hide from me." He strikes the door. "You cannot fight me." He strikes the door again, and it begins to cave inwards.

I can't see anything! How can I get out of this if I can't see?

"I will be the end of you!" Another blow. "I will take your soul!"

I only have one choice. I have to be quick.

"And soon I will be FREE!" he shouts, his voice echoing all throughout the lockers as he strikes the door for a final time, breaking it.

With a scream I launch myself out of the locker, kicking the Dullahan in the chest. He stumbles and takes a few steps backwards. I take no time to catch my breath as I run down the hallway. The corpses that minutes ago had flooded the room now were nowhere to be seen. As I race away from the Dullahan, I pray that I can reach the doors fast enough. A flash of pain overtakes my left side. The snap of a whip fills my ears. I stumble but continue onwards, fighting through the pain.

I see the doors that lead out of this room and with every step they grow closer. Behind me, the Dullahan roars with fury as the roof is torn away above us. I look up to see an eclipsed sun behind several large tornados. I continue to run, praying to whatever God is listening to help me, to let me live another day.

"Dive!" Finnan's voice screams in my ear.

I feel the air behind me grow hot and dive to the floor. As I do, the Dullahan's whip soars overtop me, right through what would've been my heart. As the whip is pulled backwards, I scramble off the floor and continue to run. The doors are just a dozen feet away, I could feel my legs burning with effort as I race towards them.

"Aaron Ward!" the Dullahan bellows, "I will never stop hunting you! Never stop haunting you!" He cracks his whip at his horses. "There is nowhere you can go that I cannot follow. Not even that bastard Finnan can keep you from me!" Again, I feel the stinging heat come from behind me and twist my body to the right, and time seems to slow.

I watch as the whip rips through the air, narrowly missing me. My body slowly spins around, and I see the Dullahan sitting on his carriage, his horses galloping fiercely after me. The Dullahan holds head in his hand, and has it raised high in the air. But of everything I see, it's his eyes that draw my attention. They are open, and searing white light pours out from them. They stare directly at mine, into my very soul. I feel the world around me begin to fade away as I meet his gaze. The white light fills my vision, until I can't see anything at all…

***

Nothing. I feel nothing. No sense of touch. No pain. Nothing. I see nothing. Smell nothing. There is nothing. All is peaceful.

***

Time has no meaning, no purpose. Even trying to comprehend how long I sank in blissful nothing was equal to counting grains of sand in a dessert. Impossible. Just endless, peaceful, joyous nothing.

***

Something happened. I don't know what, or how to describe it. Just, something. Repeatedly. Rhythmically. Urgently. What is it? Why is it? Why does it disturb my peaceful nothing?

I feel nothing. Feel. Yes. Feel. That's what's happening. I feel something. But what?

Pain? No.

Sadness? No.

It continues for eternity. Maddeningly so.

The rhythm grows rapidly. The urgency too.

What is happening? Make it stop.

***

My eyes open wide, and I gasp for air. I sit bolt upright. And start to cough as air fills my lungs once more. For several minutes that is all I do, just breathe. The air stings my lungs at first, but eventually stops. Having finally caught my breath, I look around, seeing that I am still in the morgue. My heart pounds in my chest, bouncing of my rib cage painfully.

I try to stand, but collapse under my own weight, hitting the ground with a loud thud. My body is drained of energy, as though I hadn't ever moved a muscle before. My throat is dry, and I start to cough as I attempt to lift myself up off the floor again.

Black spots dance in my eyes. Again, I collapse. I have no energy; I can barely move my arms without feeling winded. As I lay on the floor, I feel wet and sticky. I look down to find a large gash just under my left ribcage. Blood flows freely from the wound.

My heart continues to beat rhythmically. Without much else to do, I begin to drift back to sleep. The sound of my heart beating lulling me to sleep like a lullaby.

***

I listen intently before opening my eyes again. All around me, I hear what sounds like people praying. Heat scorches my skin and I feel no clothes on me. Wind howls in my ears and sand finds its way in to my mouth. My hands and feet are numb. Finally, I open my eyes, revealing a crowd of hundreds stretched out before me.

They are all lower than me, as I seem to be raised up high in the air. The people below are dressed in old clothes, like robes and dresses of peasant folk. I seem to be in a dessert, as besides all the people, all I can see is sand. I attempt to move my body, only to feel a jolt of pain. I look to my left and find only more horror.

My left hand is nailed to a cross. Thick, black blood drips slowly from my fingers. I look to my right to find the same situation. Confused, I look back to the crowed of people. In the center of the crowd is a pair of shadows. Their faces are pure darkness, but they stare right at me. A woman in front of the shadows lifts her head up and her eyes meet mine.

"He is awake!" she shrieks gleefully.

The crowd stirs from their prayers and begin to shout at me with joy and hate. Closest to me, a man wearing black holy robes looks up to me and smiles wickedly. He raises is hand to the crowd of people, who all fall silent.

"The sinner wakes, and the time for repentance begins," the man says. "The time has come for us pray for his soul, so that our lord and savior, Jesus Christ, may indeed show him mercy."

The crowd then falls to their knees. The feeling in my hands begin to return as I writhe, desperately trying to free myself. I try to shout, and my voice fails me. The man in black robes, whom I assume to be a priest of some kind, begins to chant.

"Our Father, who art in heaven, hallowed be thy name." The crowd is silent as the priest's words fill the air. "Let this ungrateful sinner be guided in his final moments towards your eternal and warm embrace. Let this sinner confess his sins to you, oh Lord, so that you may in your infinite compassion and strength forgive them. Let he be protected from the devils' words and shown the truth in your scriptures, oh Mighty Lord!"

Far out in the distance, I see a large storm making its way towards me. Lightning cracks within its clouds and rather than hearing the distant echo of thunder, the chilling crack of a whip takes its place. Tears start to fall down my face as the priest continues his prayer. Desperately, I start to tug on my hands. The nails that hold me to the cross refuse to budge. The cracking of the Dullahan's whip fills the air and I look on to see the storm moving ever closer to me. The feint snorting of horse's carries its way over the sand.

I can't die here, not like this!

I start to pull, throwing all my strength into my left hand, tearing the flesh of my hand free from the nail, which remains fixed in the bloody cross. I begin to do the same to my right hand as the people below look on and scream in terror at me. A man grabs a stone and throws it at me, breaking one of my ribs. My right hand comes free, and I fall from the cross.

I hit the ground and find myself now in the middle of a snow storm. The wind stings my eyes as the cold pierces me. I attempt to stand only to fall, sliding down a snow-covered hill. I tumble and roll till I suddenly stop as I smash into a large boulder. I cling to it tightly, my skin freezing to its surface. My naked body trembles pitifully as all the heat within me is sucked away. I try to see around me, but am only blinded by white, cold light.

I feel a hand reach out and push me. I scream as I start to fall farther down what I now know to be a mountain. My skin, raw and bloody, begins to tear away as I fall farther away.

Oh, God just let me die!

In an instant, I'm no longer tumbling down a mountain, but instead falling through the air. The wind howls past my ears as I fall. The cold ebbs away, although only just. I look down and see water rising to meet me. Steam rises off its surface, and it stings my eyes as I plunge head first into its warm, dark depths. I sink for a couple minutes.

This is it, this I how I die. Just like my dad...

Panic at the thought fills me, and I desperately start for the surface of the water. The warmth fills me with renewed strength. The more I swim, the stronger I feel. My skin, thoroughly raped and raw, begins to heal. The wounds on my hands and on my side close with an itchy, tingling sensation. My head breaks the surface of the water, and I feel reborn. I gulp down water as my throat protests with pain. I drink until I cannot drink any more, my stomach starting to weigh me down with how much I've drunk. I look around, spinning in circles as I look for any land to take refuge at.

Suddenly, a loud horn bellows out from all around me. And from the depths of the water beneath me, a large shadow rises to meet me. I brace myself for impact as the mass tears through the water and lifts me high into the air. I find myself standing on the deck of an old pirate ship.

"Ahoy there, Aaron!" Finnan hollers in his thick Irish accent. The massive ship falls to the surface of the water, sending waves greater than skyscrapers in all directions. He leans forwards, griping the steering wheel of the ship tightly, "I figured you could use a ride!"

"Oh, thank fuck." I collapse on the deck of the ship.

He steps away from the wheel and rushes towards me. When he reaches me, he extends a hand. I take it and he pull me up off the deck, into a hug. I didn't realize how much I missed him. He claps me on the back, as I break away from him. I notice the silhouette of a person standing in the doorway of the captain's cabin.

"Who's that?" I ask, pulling away from Finnan.

"Ah, don't be worrying yerself now." He puts an arm around my shoulder and leads me over to the side of the ship. "Let's talk about you."

***

I tell Finnan everything I've been through in this latest series of nightmares. The padded room, the morgue, the crucifixion. How someone pushed me off the mountain. Through it all, he listens intently, his sharp blue eyes never leaving me as he hangs onto every word. When I'm finished, I ask him where he's been.

"What do ya mean, 'Where have I been'" He mocks, "I been looking for you, ya eejit!"

"Looking for me?"

"Well duh! Ya think I could just magically appear at yer side whenever I want?"

"Um, kinda yeah." I say sheepishly.

"Oh lad, haven't ya been payin' attention?" he shakes his head. "I don't have that kind of power here, no one does. 'Cept maybe yourself."

"But I heard you. Back in the morgue. If you hadn't told me to dive the Dullahan would've killed me then and there."

"I don't remember anything like that." Finnan caresses his beard. "You sure it was me ya heard?"

"Who other Irishmen do I know?"

"Shit lad, I dunno. But I'm tellin ya, it weren't me." Finnan's voice fails to mask his frustration.

"Well, what about the mountain? Who pushed me off?"

"I don't know, you sure someone pushed ya?"

"Of course! What, you think I imagined it?"

"Well technically boyo, this whole conversation is yer imagination at work." He chuckles. I frown at him, and he stops. "Listen lad, I don't know who pushed you, but it wasn't I."

"Then who did? My dad?" Finnan goes silent after I mention my dad. He turns his head away from me. "Finnan?"

"Lad, I'm sorry to say, your old man, he's…" He looks to me, his face welling with sorrow.

"What are you talking about? My voice rising. "You mean he's…"

"Gone boy, he's gone. For good this time."

"But, but he's already dead. How he can he die again?"

Finnan sighs. "It's the same reason he and I are the only one's ye've seen." Far out in the distance, the Dullahan's whip echoes out. Finnan's eyes go wide, and he turns to a shadow at the helm of the ship. "Full speed ahead! Get us the fuck outta here!"

The ship suddenly and violently lurches forwards, sending me stumbling. I catch myself on the side of the ship and sit down. Finnan sits beside me, and together we watch the ship come alive with dark shadows of men as they run around and hoist the sails. The shadow men look exactly like those I had seen at my crucifixion.

"Finnan," I look to his face, "those shadows. Who are they?"

"What them?" He looks away from me, watching the shadow men intently. "Just projections. I summoned them to keep me company. They serve as me crew."

"Company? What you mean you can talk to them?"

"Not really." He sighs. "They are just shells. Shadows, if you would." He smiles at that. "But I pretend they are old friends from my life every so often. Keeps me from going too crazy."

I nod my head and look towards the shadow men runny about the ship. But something doesn't feel right about them. I thought about the two I saw at my crucifixion, and just a soon my thoughts turned to my dad.

"Finnan, what happened to my dad?" I ask him solemnly.

He looks at me, his brow heavy. "Lad, you told me that back in that morgue of yers, you looked at the Dullahan's eyes." I nod my head. "That its son, that's what happened to him."

"Stop giving me half answers already, what happened to him?" I shout at him; Finnan tilts his head back.

"The Dullahan is a demon, or devil. Whatever he is, he needs to feed just like anything else. While you and I, when I was alive anyway, eat food and drink water, he eats the souls of those poor bastards unfortunate enough to cross his path."

"He eats souls? Seriously?"

"Yes, seriously! Gods, boy, you sure are skeptical for someone who nearly had his eaten as well."

"Wait, he nearly ate mine? Just from looking at his eyes?"

"Yes. Honestly when you told me that I thought you must've been lyin'. As far as I know once you look in his eyes, yer done for." I hang on that for a moment.

"How did I survive then?"

A dark look flashes across Finnan's face for a second. Quickly replaced by what felt like feigned wistfulness.

"I don't know." He runs his hand through his thick, red beard. "Maybe ya didn't."

"Huh? What do you mean?" I start to panic.

"Calm down, will ya!" he groans. "Gods, lad, you sure are jumpy."

"What do you mean I might not have survived?" I ask, frustrated at Finnan's carefree response.

"I mean, maybe he did get yer soul. A piece of it at least."

"A piece?"

"Yeah." Finnan continues to scratch his beard. "There was this belief, back in my day, that the soul wasn't a single thing. But multiple pieces."

"Multiple pieces," I scoff, "and you think the Dullahan got one of them?"

"It's just a theory." He holds his hands up. "But if I'm right, that means you might have a way of stayin' alive a bit longer. Although everyone else I met here went on the first go." He snaps his fingers. "Just like that."

"So back there, at the swamp, my dad, he…"

"Yep. Your Da did a good job holding that shadowy cunt back long enough for you and me to get away."

"So, it's just me and you left?" I ask.

"Well, and yer nephew."

I glare at him.

"Just making sure you remember what yer fighin' for."

"So, do you know how I can stop him? Any ideas?"

"It's like I been sayin,' lad." Finnan stands up. "Ya can't beat this fucker. He's too strong."

"But I control the dream, you told me that. And I have; the door at the padded room, my wounds that are healing."

"I'm sorry, lad, but that's about all ye be able to do. I been around for centuries, and I seen a lot. Everyone of yer ancestors have tried to fight and every one of them failed miserably. Not one of them could do more to him than run and pray for another day."

On that grim note, I stand up and lean against the ship's rail again, overlooking the water. Although we are racing through it, the water below is motionless. Not a wave in sight and from this angle it looks like glass.

Finnan leans beside me.

"How have you stayed ahead of him?" I ask. I look over and catch a startled expression fleeing from his eyes.

"Whatcha mean?" he replies curtly.

"You said he wants to eat our souls. How have you stayed ahead of him for centuries?"

Finnan starts to stroke his beard again.

"You can't wake up to get away from him, so I just don't understand how you're still here?"

"Well, you see, lad." Finnan takes a short pause as he thinks of an answer. "The Dullahan isn't that interested in me. At least, not yet. I'm already dead and as ya said, I can't escape into the real world like you can." He looks back out over the ocean. "But once every last one of our line is gone, I'm sure he will do whatever it takes to finish me off. If he hasn't already."

"So, you are content with just running away while your family fights and dies at the Dullahan's hands?"

"It ain't so easy, lad." Finnan sighs. "As I said, you can't fight him. And in case you didn't notice I've saved your life a few times now, so I ain't exactly doing nothing."

We stand in silence for a while, thinking about what each other has said.

Fighting is apparently impossible. The Dullahan always wins according to Finnan. My best chance is just to run and hope I live long enough for Jake to live a happy life. Why? Just so he can be butchered in his forties instead of as a kid?

"I have to try; I can't do this forever Finnan." I look to him, "I can't just let this fucking curse or whatever this is continue onwards."

Finnan hangs his head. "Then I guess you'll be just another fool I have to watch die." He spits.

"I guess so."

We both stay there, quietly. I look back at the crew or shadows, watching them run about the ship, trying to maintain the speed. It's almost amusing, there is no wind, yet the sails are taught as the ship glides through the water. The snap of a whip fills the air, sending shiver though my spine.

I look back at the water, to see ripples coming towards the ship. As they bounce off the hull, the ripples grow in intensity, becoming waves. The sun, which beat down fiercely upon us now grows dark as storm clouds blanket the sky. I look towards the horizon and see a small shadow making its way towards the ship. From the shadow comes the rhythmic flash of light as the Dullahan cracks his whip.

"Hey, Finnan."

"I see 'im." He spits again, "The cunt has found us."

The Dullahan races towards the ship, his carriage only a mile or so away. His voice rings out over the rapid waves as lightning tears through the sky, illuminating the tornados the follow in the Dullahan's wake.

"Aaron Ward!"

I look to Finnan, who stares intently out at the Dullahan. "What do we do?"

Finnan sighs and stops leaning on the ship, "Looks like it's time for you to wake up." Faster than I could see, Finnan punches me in the chest, knocking the wind out of my lungs. I collapse to the floor of the ship, gasping for air.

I start to lose consciousness and air refuses to enter my lungs. My vision turning black, the last thing I hear is the Dullahan screaming out, "Finnan, you old coward! I'll get that boy soon enough. And after I'm done with him, I'll be coming for you!"

Chapter 8

My eyes snap open and my back arches as I awake. I gasp for air, drawing in breath greedily. The stiches on my chest burn with the effort of holding my chest together as my lungs struggle for air. I lay like this for a couple minutes. My bed is damp for some reason, and I start to wonder why. Then the realization of all that's happened hits me.

Finnan. Is he gone now, too?

I sit up on the bed and look to my side. Where the Dullahan's whip had cut me there was now a long, fresh scar. The skin was dark brown and taught, as though it could reopen at any time. The palms of my hands are no different; thick globs of scar tissue stretch across my palms and back of my hands. I clench my fists and, to no surprise, find that I struggle to bend my hands. The scar tissue is thick and awkward.

Guess that's better than nothing.

My stomach grumbles angrily. I start to wonder how long I've been asleep as I get myself dressed. I grab my phone and check the time.

What?

The time on my phone reads nine o'clock. I mustn't have slept that long; it wasn't even four when I went to sleep. But that's not what is so shocking. I had been released from the hospital on September 13th, but according to my phone, it was now September 15th.

Did I sleep for two days?

My door opens suddenly, and I find my sister Chloe standing in the doorway.

"Oh, thank God!" she sighs and looks over her shoulder, shouting into the hallway, "Mom, he's awake!"

She steps into the room and gives me a furious look. "What the hell?"

"What, what'd I do?" I ask, slipping my phone into my pocket.

"You've been asleep for two days, you bum. We thought you might've slipped into a coma."

My mom appears at the doorway. She smiles and rushes towards me, pulling me into a hug. "Oh, thank God that you're ok!"

"Yes, I'm ok." I push her off me. "I was just tired, ok? I guess I slept a little longer than I planned."

"Slept?" Chloe quips. "No, you weren't asleep. We tried waking you up. I even threw a glass of water on your face. Nothing."

That explains the bed.

"I started shaking you, but you wouldn't wake up," my mom says. "I was just about to call a doctor when Chloe heard you were awake."

I sit back down on my bed. "I'm sorry you guys worried. I didn't mean to scare you. I must've been just really tired. After all, I didn't sleep at all in the hospital." I look to my mom, and see her eyes are full of concern, "But I promise you, I'm fine."

"Aaron, tell me right now what the fuck is going on with you!" Chloe demands.

"Nothing," I lie, "Like I said, I was just tired."

Chloe doesn't believe me for a second. Just as she is about to continue arguing with me, my mom comes to my defense. "Chloe, he went almost a whole week without sleeping in that hospital. Now I don't know why he did but I'm just glad he finally got some sleep."

"But Mom, don't you think that that's insane?" Chloe half shouts. "He doesn't sleep for a week after nearly dying in a fucking alleyway and now he sleeps for two days straight. It's really concerning, and I'm shocked you aren't bothered by it at all!"

"If something was going on, I trust Aaron would tell me," Mom reassures her. "If there was any way we could help, I'm sure Aaron would let us know. But not sleeping and then sleeping for a long time afterwards is normal, especially for teenage boys."

Chloe shakes her head in disbelief, "Whatever. If you guys don't want to tell me what's happening, fine. I don't care anymore."

Frustrated, Chloe storms out of the room. With a deep sigh, my mom sits on the end of my bed. Her eyes fall to my hands, they grow wide at the sight.

"Oh God! Aaron!" She takes my hands in hers. "What happened?"

I pull my hands away from her, "It's nothing, I'm fine."

"Aaron for God's sake! You aren't fine!"

"Mom, this is what it is. I'm working on fixing it." I look into her eyes. "Just, trust me, ok?"

"Aaron, I don't understand what is happening with you." Tears start to form in the corners of her eyes.

"I know, Mom," I lean forwards and pull her into a hug, "But I'm figuring it out. I promise, I'll fix it."

She's silent. I know she wants to ask more, but she doesn't. She pulls away from me, kissing my forehead, before getting up and making her way for the door. She stops at the doorway, "Are you gonna be leaving for your Aunt Claudia's?"

"Yes." I reply, curtly.

She sighs and leaves the room.

***

After a quick bite to eat, I get into my car. I go to turn the key, stopping as my eyes catch onto Zoë's house. I stare at her front door for a while. I want so desperately to go to her door. To demand that we talk about things. About Deacon, about us. More than anything else, I want to tell her what has been happening to me. I want her to come with me, as though she could help me.

Instead, I turn the key and start the car, beginning my long drive to Gladstone, Michigan.

***

As I drive, I think about a lot of things. First, my dad. I don't remember much about him. I remember what he looked like, what he sounded like. The clothes he wore. But as for what he actually did with me, almost nothing. I start to feel angry.

Why can't I remember anything about him? What was his favorite food? What did he do for work? What were some of his hobbies? Did he like movies? Sports? Woodworking for fucks sake? I can't remember ever doing anything with him. I don't know if we ever did anything. Was he already dealing with the Dullahan when I was born? Is that why I don't remember him?

The Dullahan. That fucker. Why does he have to kill us, huh? I mean, what did we do to him? My dad, my uncle, my cousin Brian. Now me. And after me, Jake. What did a 4-year-old do to deserve this?

I ranted and raged in my head for hours about the Dullahan. The more I thought about things, the angrier I got. Then my thoughts shifted to Deacon and Zoë.

What does she see in that bastard? I mean I get it; she doesn't like me that way, fine! But him? A sleezier, more manipulative piece of shit you've never seen. All he wants is to get in her pants, fuck everything else. And if she likes him so much, why doesn't she let him then? No, instead she has to play hard to get with him all the while stringing me along. Of course, she doesn't have those feelings for me, who the fuck would? And yet she picks him. Mr. Stereotypical Scumbag. MOTHERFUCKER!

As I fumed, my anger slowly started to eb away into sadness and despair.

What if I can't win? What if, I really can't beat the Dullahan. Or stop the curse. Maybe my only choice is to try and survive for as long as possible and try to give Jake as happy a life as I possibly can. Or should I just let myself die. Let Jake die too and let that be the end of it. But what if the Dullahan doesn't stop with Jake? What if he goes on to another person? Chloe? Mom? Aunt Katrina? Or hell even another family line? Start the cycle all over again.

And what about Zoë? Are we even still friends anymore? Can we ever be again if not? Will she stay with Deacon? What if she never sees him for who he is? For whom I know him to be? What if he hurts her? Or worse, what if he doesn't? Maybe he actually cares for her. Maybe he'll marry her. Make her truly happy.

The thoughts start to make me sick. I pull over to the side of the road, the sky black above me. I step out of the car and put my hands above my head, breathing in the crisp night air. I start to stretch my body and feel all my bones crack satisfyingly. I make my way back to the car. As I reach out for the door handle, I hear the familiar sound of horses galloping, followed closely by the snapping of a whip.

No. No, I'm awake, he can't be here!

The sounds grow closer and closer, echoing out all around me. I look down the road to see two bright white orbs fast approaching me. I scream with fear as I dive into the car.

No no no no no! I'm awake. I'm awake. I'M AWAKE!

The lights are right in front of me, and I shield my eyes desperately.

"I'm awake!" I scream. The light bleeds through my eyelids. As I prepare to face my death, a truck horn blares out. My eyes snap open in time to see the large freight truck barrel past me. My car shakes slightly as it passes. Then it's gone, just as fast as it appeared. My body goes limp in my seat, my breath heavy. After a moment, I start to laugh uncontrollably.

God that was dumb!

I laugh for a while; tears start to stream down my increasingly red face. After a while, I finally compose myself.

I'm fucking losing my mind.

***

It was late at night by the time I entered Gladstone, or just very early in the morning depending on your point of view. I figured rather than bothering my ancient great aunt at two in the morning I'd better find a motel to crash. Despite not wanting anything to do with sleep, I knew that if I was gonna get to see Aunt Claudia, I'd need to be as well rested as I could be. After paying the overworked night shift employee behind the counter, I was given the key to room number 13.

Of course, room 13. Just had to be the one number associated to bad luck and evil.

I get to my room and am surprised to find it isn't too disgusting. The walls are white, as though freshly painted. The beds are made up with bleached white pillows and blue sheets. The room smells lightly of lavender. I go ahead and check the bathroom. White tile floors and baby blue walls, basic as most bathroom go.

After a quick shower, I make my way to the bed. I set my phone alarm for six hours from now and pray that I'll be lucky enough to wake up to it. I lay back in the bed and sink into the unnecessarily fluffy pillow. I stare up that the ceiling, watching the fan spin away. And drift off to sleep…

***

The sun beats down on me. I try to cover my face with my hand, only to find that my hands are restrained.

No! Not again!

I look at my hands, squinting under the harsh sun, and see thick chains strapping them down. My legs are, too. I look around as best I can and see that I'm chained to a large rock. The sound of waves crashing tell me I'm by water. I waste no time trying to pull myself free, but like the cross, find myself drained of all energy.

Suddenly, from high above me, a large shadow passes over me. I look to the sky, squinting desperately trying to keep the light from my eyes. The shadow passes my vision again, but only for a second. This time, the shadow is accompanied by the caw of a bird.

A vulture!

The shadow passes over me again, and the caw of the vulture rings out once more. I start to strain myself against the chains, praying to just rip my arm free. Out of nowhere, the vulture lands on me, its large talons piercing the soft flesh of my stomach. I start to wriggle and writhe, trying to make the vulture fly away.

The vulture is unfazed and stares down at me hungrily. With a swift peck, it digs its beak into my cheek. I grit my teeth in pain and continue trying to pull my arm free. The chain doesn't give. The vulture pecks me again, this time taking a small chunk of my cheek with it. It gobbles down my skin and, despite the immense heat from the sun, a chill runs down my spine, sending shivers all throughout my body.

As I shiver, the vulture takes another bite out of my face, this time ripping away a much larger part of it. I start to cry from the pain and continue to strain against the chains. They refuse to budge. I start to imagine the chains as weak as dental floss. Just tiny bits of string. They start to give a little under my effort. Then the vulture takes another bite out of my face. Only this time, it takes my left eye along with it!

I scream out, arching my back and writhing in pain. The vulture starts to flap its wings and digs its talons deeper into my stomach. Anger starts to fill my body again, and I continue to pull against the chains with all my might. All the while imagining them ripping apart like paper. The vulture goes to take another peak at my face, just as my arms rip free of the chains. I roar with fury, and I grab the vulture by both parts of its beak.

The vulture tries to fly away, but I hold onto it. With all my strength I start to pull its beak apart, opening its mouth. It caws out in a panic as its jaws stretch wider and wider. Eventually, I hear it choke as its beak begins to snap and crack under the pressure. The vulture twists its head desperately trying to break my grasp on it. But nothing stops me as, bit by bit, the vulture's beak is ripped open.

The lower jaw rips away violently, taking with it a large chunk of its throat. Blood flies out, coating me. Some gets into my open mouth, and the taste of copper and salt bathes my tongue. The lower jaw falls away from me and the vulture, held firmly in my hand, looks at me. My one eye meets its gaze as I watch, with sickening glee, as the filthy scavenger's life flees from its body. I drop it onto the ground and let myself slide down the face of the rock to which I was chained.

My feet hit the solid ground beneath me, and I look around. All around me is endless sea. I find myself standing on a small cluster of rocks, waves gently colliding with them. The sky above is clear, not a cloud in sight. The sun beams down at me, as though it was trying to melt me.

My face starts to burn, and I inspect the damage. I feel my face and notice on the left side, from the base of my chin up to my brow, that the skin has been thoroughly ripped away. The muscle and tendons that normally lay underneath stretch and contort uncomfortably. Some of the muscle has been damaged, too, and I realize I cannot properly open my jaw. I inspect the spot on my stomach where that vile bird landed. The marks where its talons punctured the skin are starting to swell and blood begins to flow steadily.

I make my way to the edge of my rocky island and fall to my knees before the water. The waves kick up little droplets of water and they land on my face. It stings slightly, but not enough to make me suspect salt water. With the heat beating down on me, I lower my hands and bring up a small pool of water to my lips. I drink deeply and am thankful to whatever God there is that the water is fresh and cold.

Without any restraint, I fall on my hands and let my head fall through the water's surface. I gulp water down, imagining myself draining the sea of every last drop. And before I realize it, that's exactly what happens. After drinking for what only feels a couple of minutes, the water vanishes.

I open my eyes, and look around, hoping to find where the water might've gone. Instead, I am dismayed to see in place of the water that I had so childishly taken for granted was now pure white sand. Sand that stretched onwards forever in every direction. I figured nothing could be worse than the morgue or the padded room.

Oh, how wrong I was.

Without seeing another choice, I preceded to jump off my rocky sanctuary and began to walk forwards into the unknown.

***

I walked for days, the sun never once feeling the need to give me reprieve. No clouds in the sky to offer me shelter, no night to come and cool the air. Just endless heat. I walked on, desperately hoping that maybe I'd find a puddle of water that had been left behind. Or perhaps maybe some shelter to rest in.

As I walk, I feel myself begin to hallucinate. Shadows of Brian and my dad appear and disappear within blinks of my one eye. I start to cry.

Is this what they went through? Did they suffer this badly? Or worse?

My face began to throb with pain, as did the wounds on my stomach. Dark scabs had begun to form over them, and the skin surrounding them had turned to a reddish hue. I imagined my face was of similar condition.

Is that how I'll die? Infection?

On and on I walk. All I had to protect me from the heat and sand was a tattered pair of shorts. No shirt, no shoes.

No service.

I chuckle to myself at my stupid joke. Delirium is clearly starting to set in. I need to find a way out of this dessert. I need water. More than anything I need to wake up. But I can't.

Finnan. Where are you when I need you?

That isn't fair. It seems I always need him. Or help of some kind. How can I hope to survive if I can't depend on myself? My mom, my dad, Zoë, a hospital doctor, and now Finnan. How pathetic. A crack rips through the air and a bolt of lightning tears through my heart. I stop walking, and slowly turn around.

There before me was the Dullahan. His carriage was nowhere to be seen, but I figured it had to be close by. The Dullahan held his whip in his right hand, his head in his left. His eyes were closed tightly. He wore a long black coat. As though the heat didn't bother him. His clothes seemed to be made from pure darkness. Rippling and emanating from him in whisps.

"Aaron Ward, Son of David," he speaks calmly, no malice in his voice, "You are supposed to be dead."

I crack a smile at that. My face throbbing with pain as I do.

"Sorry." I croak, my voice breaking. "Didn't seem that fun."

The Dullahan sighs, and his shoulders sag slightly.

Is he tired?

"Why…" My voice breaks.

"Why am I trying to kill you? Because that's the price of the pact," the Dullahan states.

"I didn't make any pact with you." My legs begin to wobble.

"I know, the price you're paying is unfair and cruel. I don't enjoy taking your life." He raises his head, meeting me at eye level. "I'm certainly impressed by you. Not one before you has ever managed to survive looking into my eyes. It shows strength. But also makes me think you had help."

"Help from who?" The longer I stand still the more my legs shake, ready to give out. "I haven't seen anyone but Finnan and my dad, and you've killed them."

"I killed them?" The Dullahan chuckles. "I killed your father yes, many years ago now. But Finnan, the last two times he's stood in my way he managed to save you. But he's not here this time." The Dullahan gestures to the desert. "No sea for him to sail on. No place for him to rob me of what I earned."

"Finnan's alive?" My one eye goes wide with shock. "But I-"

I'm interrupted by the Dullahan as his eyes open. Bad timing for him as just when the light of his eyes reaches me, my legs have already given out from beneath me. I collapse to the ground and bury my face into the sand. All over, my nerves fire, trying to get me to stand up and run. My face feels as though the vulture was ripping it apart all over again. The Dullahan curses, and the snap of a whip follows a flash of pain that rips through my back.

"Stand up, Ward," he hisses. "This is not the way a Son of David should go."

Again, his whip cracks against my back, tearing the skin open. My body lies limp in the sand. I cannot move, even if I wanted to.

"Get up!" he shouts at me, slamming his whip into me with all his might.

I feel nothing; I'm too tired for pain.

"Get up!" he shouts again, slamming his whip into me, over and over again. "Is this how you want to die? Curled up in the sand, whipped to death like a filthy peasant?"

I want to shout at him, want to charge him, tackle him to the floor and beat him into the sand. I want to grab that fucking whip of his and split his stupid fucking head in two. I want nothing more than to make him suffer, as he has made me suffer. But I cannot. I'm too weak.

"Your father would be ashamed of you if he saw you now," the Dullahan spits at me.

At the mention of my father, what little strength I have left with me flares to life. I feel the sand beneath me begin to twist and spin. I picture a vortex forming, ripping apart the ground. And so, it does, the ground splitting open in between me and the Dullahan, separating us. I lift myself off the desert floor and face him.

"A chasm," the Dullahan grunts, "That's the best you can do?"

The wind begins to howl, sending up the sand around us. The air quickly became dusty and all but impossible to see through. Through the wind, the Dullahan started cracking his whip, flashes of light emanating from where he stands.

"Enough running and hiding, Ward!" his voice thunders. "You can conjure up as many storms as you wish. As many chasms and doors as you can imagine! But I will find you in the end!"

I didn't start the storm. So, who did?

A flash of light followed by the snap of a whip tears through the air right before me. It just misses me, the end of the whip sailing right over my left shoulder. The speed in which the whip cut through the air seemed to kill the wind, and the sand falls from the air all at once. Now face to face with the Dullahan once more, he smiles at me. He raises his whip, ready to bring send it right through me. I try to force my body to move out of the way, but I have used up all my strength just getting off the ground. I am helpless as the whip starts to sail through the air right for my face.

Suddenly, the temperature drops. The sun, which moments ago roasted me in its light, disappears. The Dullahan's whip snaps centimeters from my face. Just as I'm about to die, I feel my legs get taken out beneath me, as though someone kicked the back of my knees. I fall backwards, my head thudding against the sand. The Dullahan's whip cuts the air, sending a flash of light as it connects with the spot that moments ago my face resided. The sand digs into the open flesh on my back, and I feel as though I'm on a bed of nails. As the Dullahan's whip returns to him, I look up to the sky, which has gone dark, almost black. The air is freezing now, my breath fogging as it leaves my mouth.

"What are you doing?" the Dullahan shouts. "Stop fighting already!"

The darkness seems to grow closer and closer, as though I am to be buried in a thick blanket of shadow. The Dullahan must see this, too, and he screams in rage.

"No! Not when I'm so close!" The darkness reaches me, sweeping me away in its icy depths.

Chapter 9

The water slams into us, pinning us to the bottom of the sea. It is followed swiftly by a strong current that lifts us up, sending us spinning away from one another. I twirl and spin helplessly while what little air I have in my lungs is forced out. Water pours down my throat and into my stomach. I hoped the water would've been clean and refreshing but am shocked instead to find it is now salty and bitter. Panic ensues and adrenalin kicks in. I start to flail and swim in every direction. But the current is too strong.

Being so deep underwater, I see nothing. No light reaches my eye. In this darkness, I feel my life begin to fade away once more. A calm overcomes me, my body falling still in the deep dark water. No sooner am I face to face with death am I forcefully pulled back towards life. I cough violently, expunging water from my lungs. Once it's gone, I lay on my back, resting for a moment. But a bright light shines hatefully down on me.

Where am I?

I sit upright, carefully looking around. I hope to see Finnan but am greeted with nothing. I sit in an empty, white room. No furniture, no decorations, nothing but pure white walls and floor. The entire ceiling is one giant light, radiating white light down on me.

I stand up and turn in circles, examining the walls. At first, I feel like I am in another padded room. Then I see the mirror, which rests on the wall behind me. I walk over to it and am surprised by what I see. Through my one good eye, I see what has become of my face.

The left side is a disaster. From the edge of my nose to my ear, from the tip of my chin to the bottom of my brow, is a nightmare in itself. The entire left side of my face is covered in large, lumpy scabs. The muscle has begun to rot and tear away, and the socket where my eye once lay now oozes puss. I started to feel light-headed and brace myself against the wall.

Come on, you can fix this!

I look back into the mirror and focus on my face. I imagine the torn, rotting muscle beginning to fuse back together and regrow, the skin stretching, and laying overtop the newly formed foundation. Finally, I imagine my eye regrowing, filling out the socket and granting me sight once more.

As my face slowly rebuilds itself, so do the wounds on my stomach. All over my nerves fire away, sending waves of stinging pain and nausea to me. But, soon enough, my face is back to normal. With a sigh of relief, I turn back towards the center of the room.

Immediately, the bright light above me turns off, leaving me in absolute darkness. The room grows cold, colder than anything I'd ever experienced before. A loud hiss fills the air as it begins to be sucked out of the room. I take as deep a breath as I can.

My cheeks puff out as I desperately try to hold the air in. The walls and floor break away revealing on the outside of the room was endless, empty space. Stars twinkle all around me as I look on in awe. The remnants of the room fall away from me, disappearing in the darkness between the stars. I watch on, drifting peacefully into space.

My lungs start to ache for air as I float in the void. All around me, the stars begin to blink out of existence. I feel a pull to my left and look to see a wall of darkness stretching out for miles. I don't know what to make of it. No inky blackness, no wispy shadows, nothing remotely defining. Just a long, empty void in space. I look around to find more stars continue to blink out of existence, adding to the ever-growing darkness. I watch in eerie silence, wondering what will happen to me next.

The last of the stars goes out, and I'm left blind and helpless in the empty void of what I believe to be space. My lungs scream for air, and I feel myself grow light-headed. I try to imagine some form of oxygen. A space suit or a mask, anything. But nothing comes to me.

Why can I make a fucking door out of a wall but can't conjure up something to help me breathe?

Light erupts from behind me. Although I have my back turned to it, what light makes its way around me burns my eyes. Something strong starts to pull me backwards towards the source of light. I twist my body, desperate to see what is source is. As I spin in the void of space, I am greeted with a most beautiful sight.

A ring of pure light stretching for miles in either direction greets my eyes. The light bends and pulses as though it's alive. A second ring of light bisects the first. The second ring bends towards me and emanating from it is a dull hum. In the center of the rings of light, is more endless darkness.

A blackhole!

All around me, the stars return, as though someone blew on the embers of a fire. The blackhole continues to pull me closer towards it. My eyes burn as the light grows fiercer. I hold my hand up to shield my eyes, only to watch in horror as my hand and arm begin to stretch and whirl. My skin swirls and warps under the immense gravitational force from the blackhole. The pain makes me shout out, but no sound fills my ears. Furthermore, no air fills my lungs.

I scratch at my throat, desperately trying to breathe, to no avail. As I fight for air, I watch as more of my body begins to stretch and warp. The blackhole is right in front of me now, if my hands were still normal, I could reach out at touch the bright ring of light that hovers just inches away above me. I look back to the center of the blackhole, and am propelled deeper into absolute darkness…

***

I hit the floor of my motel room and cough fiercely. I suck air in and am once again in tears. I lay there for a while, enjoying the noise of the fan which creaks faintly as it spins on the ceiling. I also take pleasure in the rough hard carpet that I lay on. I pull my blanket off the bed on top of me, attempting to shelter myself from the everlasting cold that has settled on my skin. There I sit for a few minutes, enjoying everything that comes with being alive.

I swear, if this ever ends, I'm going to live an entirely different kind of life.

Despite my best attempts, the cold refuses to leave me. I force myself up off the floor and make my way towards the bathroom. I flick the light on and am greeted by a pale stranger in the mirror. He's hunched over, clutching a blanket to him. His body seems thin and frail. His face is most noticeable, with pale sickly skin, frost blue lips, and a wide ridged scar across the left part of his face. The scar stretches from the tip of his chin to the top of his brow, from the edge of his nose to the lobes of his ears. It is dark brown, with a leather-like texture.

But, of everything I see, it's my eyes that concern me. My right eye is its usual, dark brown. But my left eye is not one I recognize. The white of the eye is bleached by a pink hue, the pupil small and unfocused. And the iris? Rather than a deep brown, it is instead a cloudy blue. I raise a trembling hand to my right eye, covering it, and am thankful that my vision seems to be unaffected. But my face. *How will I ever explain this? To anyone!*

I stand in front of the mirror for some time, taking in my new, disfigured appearance. Eventually the bone chilling cold forces me to the shower. After an eternity of marinating in the hot water, I finally feel warm. As I step of my shower, I look once more at myself in the mirror.

The cloudy eye and scared, leathery skin are impossible to ignore. The numerous scars from my nightmares glare up at me. My chest, from where the Dullahan first struck me with his whip, both my legs which were nearly ripped off by the force of the Dullahan's blows, my side where again the spine whip left its mark, and finally my back, which looked as though I'd just escaped from a cotton plantation in the deep south. My stomach bore the marks from the vultures' talons. As well as my hands, which barely could move as they were made up mostly of scar tissue.

I look like I just walked through hell. In some aspects, I guess I did. I wanted to feel anger but couldn't. Despair refused to grip me. And fear was nowhere to be found. I was hollow. Empty.

How can I go on like this?

Loud knocking snaps me back to reality. I quickly throw on some clothes and make my way towards the door of my room. I open it to find a large man standing before me.

"Jesus, what's with your face?" he blurts out and I rub the scar gently. "Whatever, look it's 12 o'clock. You were supposed to be out an hour ago. Either pay for another day or get the hell out."

"Sorry," I make my way back into the room and he follows me. "I lost track of time, let me just grab my stuff."

"Yeah, yeah, hurry up. I ain't got all day." He snaps his fingers.

I gather up what little stuff I have with me and leave. Back in the car, I am greeted again by my disfigured face.

"Yeah well, you never were pretty." I tell myself. I start the engine and continue my journey onwards towards Aunt Claudia's...

***

I pull my car into the driveway of a large, old house. The shingles on the roof are tattered and falling off. The paint on the outside of the house is faded and peeling, going from what was once a smooth white to a messy beige. The front door was big and painted black, with a gold doorknocker. I brace myself and knock on the front door.

Several moments pass and nothing happens. I press my ear to the door, hoping to hear something inside. Instead, I am greeted with silence. Once more I knock on the door, slamming the gold doorknocker as hard and as loud as I can. Again, silence. Seeing no other choice, I start walking back to my car.

Then I hear the clicking of a lock. I spin back around and watch as the door opens, revealing a tall dark man in casual clothing. He looks me up and down and doesn't seem to like what he sees.

"Can I help you?" he asks.

"Um, yeah I'm here to see Claudia Bell."

"Reason for your visit?" he commands.

"Do I need a reason?" The man doesn't respond, just blinks. "She's my aunt, I haven't seen her in a long time and want to check up on her."

"Got any ID on you kid?" he asks.

"Um, yeah," I fish out my wallet and hand him my driver's license. After a moment of examining, it he gives it back to me.

"Wait here, I'll go ask Mrs. Claudia if she's willing to see you." Before I can reply, he closes the door in my face.

I wait there for a few minutes, each going by like an hour. I felt my body twitching with nerves. *This was it; I might finally get some answers!* After what feels like an eternity, the door opens once more, and the man ushers me inside. As he closes the door behind me, I look around the main entrance.

The house is old, but conveniently designed, with the front entrance leading directly into the living room, which was empty and silent. Behind the living room was the kitchen, with only a large center island separating the two. The man gestures for me to follow him and leads me down a long hallway.

I see several rooms closed on either side of me as we walk. I wonder what is inside of them as the man leads me to a staircase. As we ascend, I feel compelled to speak to my guide:

"So, who are you exactly?"

"Caretaker," he says bluntly, "I do everything around here. I make sure your aunt takes her medicine. As well as cook, clean, basic household chores. Etcetera."

Judging from the outside of the house I doubt he's that diligent.

We reach the second story of the house and walk a little further down another hallway before coming to a stop before a door. The man turns and looks at me.

"She's in there. Told me that you're her nephew, so I hope I can trust you not to do anything untoward." the guy says with a commanding tone.

"Course." I nod at him.

Satisfied, he turns and walks away, back down the stairs. I watch him go before turning my attention back to the door. Hesitantly, I open the door which swings open, revealing the inside. Inside I see a small room, with a bed and an old armchair. Both fare acing the tv, which streams some lame cooking show.

Laying in the bed is my great aunt. Her gray hair all frizzled and uncared for. Her cloudy blue eyes sport deep, dark bags underneath and a large red splotch I hadn't noticed before rests on her right cheek. If it wasn't for her chest rising and falling, I'd have argued she was dead.

"Aunt Claudia?" She doesn't react to my voice. "Aunt Claudia, it's me, Aaron. We spoke after the funeral. For Brian."

Again, she doesn't react. I look around and find a remote for the tv resting on the armchair. I turn the tv off and look back to see my aunt's eyes are now firmly locked onto me.

"You saw him, didn't you?" she whispers.

So, she does know about the Dullahan! Relief washes over me. *I'm not crazy!*

"The Dullahan?" I ask her.

"You know his name?" she blurts out, looking shocked.

"Yeah? Should I not?"

"No, it's very strange." She starts to sit up. "How'd you discover it?"

"He told me."

"Did he now?" She seems impressed by this. "That means you're special. Everyone else I know of whom he's hunted only discovered his name by looking back on our history."

"That's why I'm here," I say, "I need to know everything I can about him."

"You wish to try and fight him?" She raises her voice, and I fear it will break on her.

"I just want to know if I can stop him."

"You can't!" she wheezes. "He cannot be stopped, cannot be endured. He is death!"

I shake my head in frustration. "So, there's nothing you can do to help me?"

"There," she points to a closet on the other end of the room, "in there. You'll find all you need in there."

I do as she says, pulling an old, dust covered box out of the closet. I open it up revealing dozens of old papers and journals. I begin to look through it, finding at the bottom of the box a large leather-bound book. Wrapped around it is a large, gold amulet. Inscribed on the amulet are the words **Féuch an emissary an bháis.** Encircling the words are dozens of small Celtic knots. The amulet is light, and a warmth emanates from it. As I stare at it, I hear the words inscribed on them being spoken by my aunt.

"Féuch an emissary an bháis."

I turn to look at her. "What does that mean?"

"Behold the emissary of death." Her raspy voice sends chills down my spine. I look back to the amulet as she continues to speak, "The amulet is a charm, intended to protect members of our family from the Dullahan."

"Protect how?" I ask, "As in, no more nightmares?"

"Sadly, no." She sighs, "But within them it should give you the edge you need to survive a little longer."

"A little longer?" I scoff, "I don't want to just last a while longer, I want to survive! I need to survive!"

Aunt Claudia goes to speak but a coughing fit overtakes her. As she coughs, I can see the physical toll it takes on her. As her fit subsides, she appears even older and weaker than she did moments ago.

"The book," she wheezes.

I look down at it. It is a large, thick leather-bound book. On the cover it reads **Chronicles of Burke.** I look back to my aunt.

"What is this?"

"Our family history," she sighs, "passed down through our family from the first of us who suffered the Dullahan's curse. Everything we know about the it lies within it. If there is a chance for you to defeat him. It is within that book."

She erupts into another coughing fit. As she does, the caretaker opens the bedroom door. He rushes over to here and gives her a few pills and a fresh glass of water. Aunt Claudia stifles her cough and takes the pills, drinking the glass of water in its entirety before laying back down. The caretaker looks over at me.

"She's exhausted," he tells me. "Whatever it is you've been talking about is stressing her out. If you want to talk some more, you'll have to come back another time."

I nod my head in understanding. "I'll just show myself out."

The guy nods at me and I head for the doorway. Just as I'm stepping through, I hear my aunt shout after me, "Beware the one who cast this curse upon us!"

***

I sit in my car, my eyes burning as they scan the book of my family's history for any information that could help me. According to this book, I'm royalty. The descendant of the first kings of Ireland. One of which was King Uilleag de Burke. Uilleag was not a very popular king from what the book tells me. But he was certainly ambitious, craving the title of King of Ireland. But this ambition did not come without great cost. The greatest of which was the number of enemies he made in achieving it.

According to this book, he died just before his goal was achieved. From some mysterious illness apparently, although many believed he was poisoned. Seemed no one could prove it though.

Finally, the book got around to the topic of the curse. The writer of the book claimed that no one knew who started it, though it was assumed it was most likely one of the many enemies King Uilleag made in his conquest of the vast majority of Ireland. However, the writer did know the exact wording of the curse that brought the dynasty of Burke to their knees.

> ***Should a day come when a Burke sits on the throne of Ireland***
> ***Let the devil send his fiercest hunter***
> ***A headless fiend of shadow and death***
> ***Let all the men with the blood of Burke face the truest of terrors***

Let them never sleep, as the Dullahan hunts them throughout their dreams

Until the day the Dynasty of Burke lies dead and forgotten in the sands of time

So, it wasn't till one of my ancestors sat on the throne of Ireland that the curse began, sending the Dullahan on a seemingly endless hunt for every man in my family. But who was the first King of Ireland? And who cast this curse on my family?

I continue reading. According to the book, it wasn't until Uilleag's grandson sat on the throne of Ireland that the curse began. Ever since that day, every male member of our bloodline had been slain in their sleep by the Dullahan, their souls his to consume. All because one man became king. The story continues, telling me the name of the first member of my family, the first to be King of Ireland. High King Finnan Ua Briain.

Finnan. He was a king? No, not just a king, but King of all Ireland. That bastard, this is all his fault?

I continue reading, but the book doesn't tell me anything more about the curse that grips my family. Instead, it went on to tell me the stories of all the kings and High Kings of Ireland. Each of their stories ended the same way, death under mysterious circumstances. My family only held the Kingdom of Ireland for a few generations before being deposed. After that, the book ended with the question of how long it would be until our bloodline would be wiped out forever.

Frustrated, I slam the book and throw it on the passenger seat. Unbelievable, the book gave me nothing on how to defeat the Dullahan or break the curse. Except the information about Finnan. He was the one that started all of this over a thousand years ago; he brought this curse down on my family. And if I am to ever have a chance of ending this, I need to have a serious talk with him.

Chapter 10

As I drive back to Chicago, I think about what my aunt said. More specifically, I think about Finnan.

Could Finnan really be the reason all this has happened? Did he damn my family? If so, why? Why would he accept the title of king if he knew about the Dullahan? Did he not know? Did he not believe the Dullahan existed? Or did he not care?

Whatever his reasons, this is all his fault.

***

I arrive back at home late in the evening. I look to the passenger seat to see the golden amulet my aunt gave me. Even after the sun has set, it still seems to glow. I take it and put it around my neck, the heat radiating from it filling me with a strange sense of comfort. As I step out of my car, I barely close the door before my mom rushes outside to meet me.

"Aaron, thank God!" She pulls me into a tight hug. When she's done, her eyes fill wide with terror. "Your face!"

I explain what happened, everything. I tell her about my dreams, about how they started and why. I talk about the Dullahan and Finnan. The only thing I don't mention is seeing Dad. When I'm done, she seems in awe.

"Aaron, honey I…" She doesn't have the words.

"I know, but this is what it is. The only hope I have is to confront Finnan and hope he has a way of defeating the Dullahan."

"Oh sweety, please. Please, there has to be some other way, one that isn't so insane!"

"There isn't. Anything else would've been tried by those who came before me."

We stand there for a moment, silently, as neither of use knows what to say. Behind my mom, I see a man start to walk towards us. It's Zoë's father. He's tall and thin, with slicked-back blond hair. He sports a thick mustache that's beginning to turn white at the edges, accompanied by some gray stubble. His eyes are the same, stormy gray as his daughter's.

"Aaron, have you seen Zoë around?" he asks.

"Mr. St. John? No, no I haven't seen her."

"Dammit!" he scratches the back of his head. "I haven't seen her since Tuesday."

When we fought.

"Where did you see her last?" my mom asks.

"She was leaving for the hospital. To visit you," he says, gesturing in my direction.

"I haven't seen her since. Have you called the police?"

"Bah!" he shakes his head. "Chicago police are worthless. They probably wouldn't even look for her, let alone find her if they did."

"Well, do you have any ideas where she might be?" my mom asks.

He shakes his head.

Deacon. Could she be with him?

"What's going on out here?" Chole emerges from the house, with Jake running out from behind her.

"Uncle Aaron!" He runs up to me and hugs me.

"Zoë's missing," Zoë's dad tells Chloe.

"Missing? Have you called the police?"

"Uncle Aaron, what happened to your face?" Jake asks.

"Nothing, buddy. Hey, why don't you head on inside. Let's let the grown-ups talk." I take his hand and make my way towards the front door of my house. Chloe stops me.

"Jesus, Aaron, what the hell happened to you?"

"It's nothing."

She doesn't budge.

"Look I'm fine ok, just a stupid accident."

"Accident?" She doesn't sound convinced.

"Yes, an accident. Now can I head on in now, I'm tired."

Chloe stands in my way for a moment, looking at my face. Finally, she moves.

I take Jake inside and play with him for a bit. Apparently, Chloe just bought him some new action figures and he wanted to show them off to me. As we started playing with his toys, I felt my arms growing heavy, as though any strength I had was being sapped away. We played with them for a while, my mom and Chloe eventually joining us.

I can see they want to talk about my face, and everything else that has been happening with me lately. Chloe especially seems upset about my dismissal of my new scars. But no one talks about it. Instead, we just relax like a normal family. Soon, Jake is taken to bed by Chloe, and I follow suit. My head barely touches the pillow before I'm out cold.

***

I stand alone in the middle of a forest. The air is light and cool. The trees surround me in all directions, so thick together you can't go more than a couple feet without seeing one. They're big, stretching so high up into the air you can't tell if its day or night. I'd be cold, however the amulet around my neck seems to grow hot, filling me with warmth.

Nope. Not tonight!

I'm determined to see exactly how much of the dream I can manipulate. With enough practice, maybe I don't ever have to suffer through another horrible nightmare ever again. I take a slow, deep breath, and stare at the army of trees before me. I imagine one of them falling over, as though a strong wind would come and knock it over.

The tree before me starts to groan and creek, followed swiftly by the cracking of its truck. Then with a mighty boom, the tree comes crashing to the ground. I feel pride well up within me. I look to the other trees before me and imagine them all falling over, the exact same way. At first, nothing happens. Suddenly, a loud snap rips through the air. It is followed immediately with a loud crash as another tree falls to the ground besides me.

One after another, trees begin to topple over. Soon enough, I see the sky above. A malicious sun starring down at me. I look to the ground at the trees around me. I imagine them starting to melt away like ice into water. I picture the mossy ground I stand on becoming a solid wooden deck, like that of Finnan's ship. The trees melting away into an ocean around me.

The trees are soon enough replaced by a calm sea that stretches out endlessly. The ground underneath me erupts into what is now a large pirate ship, sitting comfortably in the ocean I have created. The sails are taught as a strong wind begins to push the ship forwards towards the horizon.

Why couldn't it have been that easy the first time?

I walk about the deck of the ship. I'm completely alone, not a soul in sight. I had imagined shadowy figures like that of Finnan's crew would be running around, tightening the sails or steering the ship. But am disappointed to find not one in sight.

I look out over the sea I have created and picture Finnan. I imagine him onboard his own ship, riding towards me on the open sea. But alas, it seems that I'm not able to make him appear at my own behest.

Is it because he's dead?

I haven't seen Finnan since the last time I was on his ship. He had sent me away, woke me up in fact, as he faced down the Dullahan. The Dullahan said that Finnan survived their fight. However, it's possible he was lying to me. After all, why would he tell me the truth?

A loud horn tears through the air. I turn around to see a large cargo ship has appeared of the other side of my ship. No sooner than it appeared does it slam into my ship which in turn makes me stumble and fall. I try to stand up, only to fall again as my ship starts to tilt towards the other ship. The cargo ship has hit mine so hard that it has cracked the hull wide open. My ship begins to rapidly sink into the sea, taking me along with it.

I try desperately to cling onto something, but there is nothing to grab. I slide off the deck and plunge into the sea below. The water is surprisingly warm, not something I had intended when making it but something I was thankful for, nonetheless. I start to swim upwards, my lungs burning for air.

I'm developing a fear of suffocation.

My head breaches the surface of the water and I drink in the stale, musty air. I look around, shocked to see that I now have appeared inside the cargo ship. I look over to see a part of the jagged, broken floor and swim over to it. As I pull myself out of the water, I examine the ship. It seems that half of it seems to be underwater, with its hull almost completely ripped apart. To my left, a set of stairs leads up, deeper into the ship. With no other choice but to dive back in the water, I start to climb.

***

I climb for hours. I'm soaked to the bone with sweat, my legs ache, and my throat is dry as sand. I look over the side of the stairs downwards, to see an endless cavern below. I look up to see the stairs going on forever. I look to my left and see another of the hundreds of doors I have passed already.

Feeling once more as if I have no choice, I open the door and enter a long, empty hallway. The lights are out, as they were in the other parts of the ship. I begin to walk down the hallway and I remember the morgue from before. I pray that there aren't any more dead people waiting to attack me.

The ship creaks and groans every so often and the air is stale and warm. I soon come across a small room. All around are hammocks and beds; I assume the crew of the ship sleeps here. *If there even is one.* I keep walking.

From behind me, I hear footsteps. I turn around, hoping to maybe see Finnan. But of course, am disappointed. Before me now are several men. Each of them big and burly, sporting thick beards and angry looks on their faces. They are dressed like they work on the ship, in overalls and work boots. One of the even has a captain's hat.

"You aren't supposed to be here," the captain says.

"Yeah, I'm not. But you guys rammed my boat so..."

"No, you were supposed to be in the forest." Another speaks. A chill runs down my spine.

"The forest?"

"He was there, waiting for you. But you made the ocean appear, you destroyed the forest he made for you." The men start to walk in unison towards me.

The captain speaks again. "Now we must keep you here."

"Until he finds you!" the men shout together before charging me.

I turn and run away from them. The long hallway which moments ago seemed endless now diverges into several other passages. I run, taking as many left and right turns as I can, hoping to lose the men. I turn again down a different hallway, only to slam into the captain. I try to push myself off him, but his grabs me by my right arm and throws me to the ground.

I struggle to get out of his grasp, Kicking him in the knee a few times. He grunts in pain as he puts more weight on top of me. The footsteps of more men approach and I look up to see the rest of the crew has surrounded me. I continue to struggle against the captain, who snaps my arm in retaliation.

"Fuck!" I holler, rage hot in my throat.

"Stop squirming; soon he will have you," The crew says as one.

"Fuck you! You damn puppets!" I spit at the boots of the nearest guy.

The ship shakes violently, forcing the crew to stumble about. The captain's grip loosens on my arm, and I rip myself free. I imagine a knife in my left hand, and it appears in time for me to plunge it into the captain's neck. I take no time to see if it kills him as I run off down the maze of hallways.

A door appears before me and I slam into it, my broken arm screaming in protest. The door opens to reveal the main deck of the ship. Fresh, salty air cools my face, but I take no time to enjoy it as I continue to run. I look over to my right to see Finnan's ship, which has somehow doubled in size from when I last saw it, has rammed the side of the cargo ship. Without hesitation, I beeline for Finnan.

The ground before me erupts and the crew of the ship climb out and onto the deck. Soon, about 30 men stand before me and Finnan's ship. The captain steps out in front of them, my knife sticking out of his throat. The men stand shoulder to shoulder. I prepare to run but am stunned by the sounds of cannon fire.

The crew is reduced to blood and ash as smoke and hellfire rain down on them. I look up to see Finnan's ship, the smoking barrels of cannons sticking out of the side of it. At the top of the ship, Finnan's red beard is unmistakable.

"Seems once more I have to save your life laddie!" he hollers, throwing a rope down the side of the ship.

I take no time to celebrate as I race for the ship, making my way up the rope as fast as humanly possible. My scarred hands grip it tightly, my broken arm burning with pain. Soon enough Finnan reaches out and lifts me over the side of the ship. I slam onto the deck as Finnan shouts for his crew of shadows to open fire. Below, the cannons begin to rip the cargo ship to pieces. Within minutes, what's left of the cargo ship sinks beneath the sea.

***

The ship moves faster than I remember, tearing through the sea. Its sails are taut as the wind propels them forward. Finnan's crew of shadowy men run about the ship in a frenzy. Finnan is at the wheel, the light of the setting sun making it seem as though his beard is lit on fire.

I stand next to him, looking out at the sea before us. I can see why someone like Finnan would choose the open sea rather than rotting in some castle somewhere. The air is salty yet refreshing. The view is astounding. The only thing I feel I'm missing is a sea shanty.

My arm throbs with pain as I take the time to fix it. A loud snap rings out in the air as the bone pushes itself back into place. The pain is immense as the bone starts to fuse back together. I feel my arm grow hot, as though the bone of my arm was made of molten metal. Finally, the heat recedes, and my arm is as good as new.

I look out over the deck of the ship. My eyes lock onto a shadow man, one of Finnan's crew. He is tightening a sail down. As he finishes, his head turns up towards me. As we stare at each other, an eerie chill runs down my spine. I break eye contact for a moment. When I look back towards the shadow man, he has disappeared. Uneasy, I turned to face Finnan.

"Finnan, we need to talk."

He doesn't look at me but clenches his jaw. "About what lad?"

"Take a guess, Your Highness." I mock.

He grips the wheel tightly. "Ah, so it seems ye finally heard that fuckin' story." He releases the wheel and takes a step away.

A shadowy man appears out of nowhere, taking his place at the wheel. The man is slightly taller than me. He's lean, though seemingly buff. I can't shake the feeling that I recognize him from somewhere.

"Yeah, I heard the fucking story. And I have to ask, why?"

"Why? Why what?"

"Why did you become king? You can't expect me to believe you didn't know what would happen? Why would you damn yourself and everyone in our family?" I shout at him.

Finnan shakes his head slowly. He looks up at the horizon, his eyes afire with the setting sun. He closes his eyes for a moment and takes a long, slow, deep breath.

"Did ya ever wonder what the name of my ship was?" he asks, still facing the sun.

"What does that have to do with this?"

"Aoibhe." He smiles at the word.

"Aoibhe?" I repeat. He turns to face me, his eyes full of sorrow.

"Tell me something,' lad. What is something that every man wants?"

I scoff at him.

"Just," he holds up his hands, "humor me."

"Power?"

"Power?" An amused looked flashes across his face. "Is that what you desire, lad?"

"No." I answer.

Finnan chuckles. "Then how can every man want it, if you don't?"

"Look, can you just get to the point!" I demand.

"A woman, lad. A woman." Finnan looks back to the sun, which has just dipped below the horizon. "Every man, whether he admits it or not, wants a woman. One whom he can share his life with," he looks back at me, "or maybe just a drink and a warm bed for a night."

"Ok, you wanted a woman, so what?"

"Aoibhe was the most beautiful woman I had ever laid my eyes on. Her hair black as the sky on a moonless night. Her eyes, as green as the grassy fields in late spring. Her skin," he holds out a hand, as though he is caressing her face once more, "so soft and fair. Flawless it was." He turns back to me. "What wouldn't a man do for the woman of his dreams?"

"You became the king for a girl?"

"Not just any girl!" Finnan exclaims. "She was the most beautiful woman I'd ever seen. Even for a princess, I was left speechless at the sight of her."

"She was a princess?"

"Yes. She was." A dark look falls back onto Finnan's face. "Back in my time, there were so many kings. So many wars. I cared for none of it. I had no ambition. I wasn't greedy. Not like my grandfather and father. Not like Aoibhe's father. They all desired to call themselves King of Ireland. All I desired was her."

"So, you damned yourself and everyone in your family, for a girl?"

"Yes, lad, and I would do so again in a heartbeat." His hand falls to his side.

"Even after the Dullahan killed you?" I raise my voice, "Even after having to watch every member of our family die in this hellish place? You'd still do it all over again?"

"How was I to know?" he shouts at me, his eyes wide and dark with rage. He takes a deep breath and speaks calmly. "How was I to know that the curse was real? Only fools would believe such shite without anything to prove their words true. I didn't fear any peasant's myth. I only cared for her."

"Yet you still became king." I challenge him. "You could've taken Aoibhe and let that be enough. But you still went on to become king. Why?"

"I wasn't supposed to be king!" he moans. He leans back against the side of the ship once more. Slowly, he slides down to the floor and whispers, "I never wanted to be king."

I kneel in front of him, "What happened, then?"

Finnan is silent for a while. I look him in the eyes, but he doesn't see me. I don't know what he sees, but I know it hurts him. His eyes begin to tear up and for a moment I consider hugging him.

"I sailed for years after I married Aoibhe." He speaks so softly. "The only thing that could pull me away from her was the open sea. But it was never for long, my love for her always called me back. For years, me and me brother and sisters lived happily. I had abdicated me claim of me father's lands to my brother. I cared not for any of it. We all had children; we were a happy family." His voice trails off.

"Then what changed?"

"Aoibhe's father, Lugaid, had finally achieved his ambitions. He was named High King of Ireland. All other kings had either bent the knee to him or lost their heads, my brothers included. With everything he'd ever wanted, he ruled for only a few years. Then his sons, Aoibhe's brothers, got sick with something. After they died, the king had no other heirs, except Aoibhe." He looks at me, tears streaming down his face. "With his sons' deaths, and his health in decline, Lugaid declared me his successor."

"So why not refuse?"

"I tried. Oh, lad I tried, I begged the king to find someone else, anyone else. But the deed was done. That night after he named me his successor, before I had even been officially dubbed King of Ireland, the Dullahan came to me. And for years on after he haunted me in my dreams." Finnan hangs his head back, "And like you and everyone that has come after me, I tried and failed to stop him." He wipes the tears away.

"Then why didn't you tell me any of this sooner?"

"What good would it have done you? The Dullahan is still hunting you. You are no closer to defeating him than you were before. All it would've done was waste your time." Finnan stares up at the night sky. Stars dancing across his eyes.

"All this because of a woman," I mutter.

"Not just any woman, lad," Finnan adds. "The most beautiful of them all."

"And it's not like we can just ask the Dullahan to stop now, can we?"

"Nah, making a deal with that devil will only bring ye more pain and misery."

Deal with the devil.

"A deal, Finnan, that's it!" I shout. His looks back at me.

"What are you on about?"

"We make a deal with the Dullahan!" I watch Finnan, expecting him to say something. He sits in silence, a pensive look resting on his face.

"What make you think he'll agree to that?" he says, his voice hollow.

"Why can't it work?"

"I don't know, son," Finnan eyes grow dark, "What if the Dullahan just decides to kill you and end things that way? Might be easier for him."

"That's not true, he's spoke to me before. Several times." Finnan tenses a bit. "Maybe he'd be willing to hear me out."

"Lad, I'm telling you it won't work," Finnan snaps.

"Why are you so intent on shutting this down?" I shout at him. "I mean, I don't see any other way of ending this, do you?"

"I can't let you die!" Finnan screams at me. The air fills with stunned silence, both of us in shock at his outburst. After a moment, Finnan speaks with a softer tone, "I seen too much of death. I can't let you die, too."

A falling star lights up the sky above the pair of us. I look up at it, the sky a brilliant haze of purple and blue as the stars shine brightly.

"Finnan, if I don't do this. I'm gonna die anyways. Either now or in 10 years, however long it takes I will die unless I can somehow stop this." I take a deep breath. "I can't go on like that. I need this to end."

The sound of the waves smacking against the side of the ship suddenly become louder. Far out in the distance, the cracking of a whip echoes from over the horizon.

"Well, even so. It seems we've run out of time together." Finnan says. I look back at him. "Yer waking up lad."

"What, no I haven't been asleep long enough."

"Don't matter, yer still waking up." A brilliant white light starts to envelope Finnan. As well as everything around me. "Until next time, lad." And everything fades away.

Chapter 11

My eyes open revealing the ceiling of my bedroom. I roll over to check my phone and am surprised to see it's nearly one in the afternoon. I drag myself out of bed, the smell of the ocean clinging to me as though I had just slept on seaweed. After a quick shower, I make my way into the kitchen, where I am greeted by Chloe.

"Hey." I say to her, but she doesn't reply, focusing instead on a peanut butter and banana sandwich.

Jake's favorite.

"Did mom make anything for breakfast?" I ask and again am ignored. "Is everything ok?"

Chloe wraps the sandwich up and tosses it into a lunch bag. She turns and without saying a word walks out of the kitchen.

"Jake, sweety! Come on let's go!" she shouts down the hallway.

"Chloe?" I tap her shoulder.

She ignores me still. She starts to pick up a suitcase right by the front door.

"Chloe!" I shout at her.

"What Aaron?" she snaps, dropping the suitcase with a loud thud. "What do you wanna talk about?"

I hold up my hands defensively. "I'm just trying to talk to you."

"About what, hm?" She tilts her head slightly. "Did you wanna talk about that nasty scar you got on your face? Or any of the scars you've gotten recently? Or how about the week you spent in a hospital? You remember, when you almost died!"

"Ok. Ok, I get it."

"Or how about your delinquent girlfriend? Have you found her yet? I'm sure she's just so eager for you to find her just so she can blow you off again."

"Ok, enough!" I shout at her. "What do you want me to say, huh?"

"I want you to tell me what the hell is going on with you!" she shouts back. "Ever since Brian's funeral you've been acting strange. You sleep for days on end. You're covered in scars which seem to appear out of nowhere. You look like you're constantly about to die. Should I go on?"

"Mommy?"

Chloe jumps and turns around revealing Jake. "Why are you and Uncle Aaron fighting?"

Chloe bends over and scoops Jake up into her arms. "Hey now, there you are goofball." She looks at me. "Me and Uncle Aaron were just having a disagreement, that's all. Nothing bad."

"Yeah buddy, nothing serious." I smile at him.

"Hey, you ready to head on over to Aunt Katrina's house?" she asks him.

"Do I have to?" he moans.

"Why, don't you wanna see her?"

"I wanted to go to the park."

"Well, there's a park by where she lives. I'm sure you find plenty of stuff to do there."

Jake looks at me. "Is Uncle Aaron coming?"

Before I can answer him, Chloe speaks for me.

"No goofball, he's not." She glares at me, "Uncle Aaron isn't feeling well again, so he can't come."

"Ok." Jake moans.

Chloe sets him down on the floor.

"Why don't you go wait in the car, ok goofball?"

"Ok." He walks over and gives me a big hug. "Bye Uncle Aaron."

I hold him tightly. Feels like forever since I got to spend the day with him. "Goodbye buddy, I see you in a little bit, ok?"

He nods and makes his way outside, closing the door behind him.

I look at Chloe. "Why are you guys going to Aunt Kat's?"

"Because her son just died." She sighs. "Look Aaron, I'm sorry, ok. But I'm worried about you, and I feel like you and Mom are keeping things from me. Things that I deserve to know about."

I nod my head. Of course, she's starting to suspect somethings up. It's damn near impossible to hide any of this from her. But I don't want to tell her what's happening. She just wouldn't believe me. Hell, she might even put me in a nuthouse.

"Look, everything's fine." I lie and she shakes her head in frustration. "I'm just going through some stuff right now. It's nothing I can't handle though, and I've almost got everything under control ok. I just need you to understand that I can't tell you or anyone about it ok?"

"Whatever Aaron," she picks the suitcase up off the floor. "Just don't expect anyone to help you if you won't tell anyone what the problem is."

And with that, she walks out the door, slamming it behind her. I sigh deeply, my side and chest hurting where the Dullahan's whip struck me.

You can't help me, Chloe. No one can.

***

I figure the best thing I could be doing is try and find Zoë. I called everyone who knew her that I could. Most of them explained how her dad had already called them and told me the same thing they told him. That not one of them had heard or seen her in over a week. I tried looking around the city at some of our old hangout spots. The school rooftops that she had somehow gotten the keys for. The old arcade we used to mess around in when we were little. The aquarium, the last place I felt any semblance of normality in my life.

It feels like it's been so long. How could it only be just a few weeks sense school got out?

I start to really worry about her. I was still a bit angry at her about our fight at the hospital, but I still cared about her. As I look for her, I think a lot about what Finnan had said to me.

Every man, whether he admits it or not, wants a woman. One whom he can share his life with...

I was pretty sure at this point that I wouldn't be sharing the rest of my life with Zoë. Hell, I wasn't sure if I'd even have a life at all. Let alone one worth sharing with someone. But even if I survived the Dullahan's curse, what chance was there of me ever being with her?

God! Why am I still thinking about that? It's not ever gonna happen, she said so herself!

And yet, she was the only thing on my mind.

***

I stand outside of Deacon's bar. It looks just as run down as the last time that I'd been here. The paint was starting to peel off the sign. The windows were cloudy and cracked. And the door screeched painfully as I entered. Looking around, I see only the bartender and a drunk patron asleep at the counter.

This is it. She has to be with him.

"Oh, it's you again," the bartender says. "I'm guessing you're looking for Deacon?"

"Yes. No!" I stammer. "I mean, I'm looking for my friend. You remember her, right, my height, blond hair, gray eyes. Seen her around lately?"

"Not that I can recall. Deacon might've though. Man's been busy lately, running all over town. Maybe she's with him."

"Is he here now?"

"No, like I said, he's been running all over town the past week. I've only seen him a couple of times."

Dammit. Now I gotta find him too.

"Well do you mind if I go up to his office?" I point to the stairs that hide behind the bar.

"I don't know you that well, kid. I'm not sure he'd appreciate that."

"Look, I'm just trying to find my friend. If she's with him, maybe the only way to find her is to find him. Hell, for all we know she could be back there right now sleeping."

"Look kid I can't jus-"

"Please. I promise I won't do anything stupid. I just need to find my friend," I beg.

"Ok, fine!" the bartender caves. "Just, go on ahead. But if you steal or break anything kid, I swear to God."

"I promise, it'll be like I was never there." I take off up the stairs and almost run face first into a door. I try to open it to find it's locked.

Over course it is. How am I going to open this?

I remember all the times Zoë talked about how her brother had taught her how to hotwire cars and pick door locks. She was always so happy and proud to show off how much trouble she could get us into. From stealing her dad's lawnmower for the robotics competition to breaking into her uncle's garage to mess around with his new crossbow he'd gotten himself.

So much stupid shit. And I'd do it all over again.

I'm about to start trying to break the door down when I remember when me and Zoë had broken into her dad's shed. I reach for my wallet and pull out the lockpick we'd used. She had given this too me after we won the robotics competition. For good luck, she said.

Good luck indeed!

It takes me a bit to get the door unlocked as I struggled to remember how to unlock a door. Zoë had taught me how to do it once but almost always she was the one getting her hands dirty. Suddenly a satisfying click sounds from inside the lock, and I open the door. It swings inwards with ease.

So, he does know how to oil a door hinge.

I walk into his office, closing the door carefully behind me. I decide to lock it, just in case. Looking around the office, I am surprised by how clean it is. Well, not so much clean as it is empty.

The room is a little big for an office. I assume it wasn't always one, maybe an apartment or something. The walls are beige white, which go nicely with the hard wood floors. The wall to my left is obscured by a cabinet. Inside is a collection of different alcohols and glasses. To my right is a large window with the shades drawn. I walk over to it and peer through them, and see the bar is directly underneath me. The window overlooks the entire lounge area.

Practical.

I step away from the window and turn to face Deacon's desk. The desk is large, made of nice solid dark wood. On the desktop rests some papers, an empty drinking glass, and a journal. Behind it is a simple door. I check it to find that it's a small bathroom. It's not as filthy as I'd expected but it isn't clean either.

Well, the guy isn't a slob like I thought he was.

I start to rummage through the papers. They're mostly bills, though it seems Deacon is actually trying to fix the bar up a bit. I'm honestly a bit shocked to see that. Deacon actually trying to be responsible? I rummage through more of the papers and find nothing else of interest. I grab the journal and begin to skim through it. Most of the entries are about the bar:

- **Dec. 14th, 2019 – Power bills are through the roof again. Not sure why the rates are so high. Need to start getting more business if this place is ever gonna be something.**

- **Dec. 19th, 2019 – Cora complained again about customers hitting on her. Apparently, they were a little more handsy than normal. Now she's going on about hiring a bouncer or something. As if I can afford that!**

You're gonna need to hire a lawyer and a new bartender if that keeps happening you cheap prick.

- Dec. 23rd, 2019 – Zoë came around again. Wanted to wish me a Merry Christmas. God, that girl is something. Everything about her screams take me, but whenever I try to make a move, she pushes me away. Sometimes I don't know what to think of her.

Huh, seems Deacon isn't Zoë's favorite person either.

I start to flip through the pages a bit. Most of the entries are about Zoë or the bar. Every so often I get something interesting.

- Feb. 17th, 2020 – Zoë dropped by today. But she brough her twink friend, Aaron. God, that guy is such a bitch. Every time I try to get in to make a move with Zoë, he cockblocks me. We were supposed to go out and get a couple of drinks on the town, but the jackass didn't have an ID!

Sorry Deacon, no drunk Zoë for you to play with.

I flip through some more pages, till finally I check his final entry:

- **143 East 44th St. 10pm!**

That last entry is circled. Obviously, this must be where Deacon is going, unless he's already been there. There's no date on the entry, but it's the only lead I've got.

The door jiggles behind me. Someone's trying to get in! I quickly close the book and try to put everything back to where I found it. Just when everything looks right, the door opens.

"What the fuck?" Deacon blurts out. I turn around and face him. "How the hell did you get into my office?"

"Hey, Deacon, look, I can explain."

"No, no, no, fuck that. I already know how you got in. You picked the fucking lock." Deacon steps into the office, slamming the door behind him.

He looks furious. As I stare at him, I take notice of his appearance. His normally closely trimmed stubble has grown out into a disheveled beard. His slicked back hair is frayed and unkempt. But what's most shocking is the large bruise on the side of his head, covering most of the left side of his face. I'd almost say he looks like me with my scar.

"Yeah, ok I did. But you weren't here, and I just needed to get in here-" I begin to explain.

"Shut the fuck up!" he points at me. "Just tell me what you want. Now!"

"I'm just looking for Zoë, I figured she might be with you so, I was trying to find you."

"And so, you decided to just break into my fucking office. You know I could kill you for this, right. Hell, I still might," he sneers.

"Look, just calm down, ok." I hold up my hands. "I'm just worried about Zoë, ok. Nobody has seen her in over a week and I didn't know where else to look for her."

Deacon scoffs. "And you think she wants to be found. Let alone by your dopey ass." I tense up.

So, he does know where she is.

"Well, I am her best friend."

"Oh please," Deacon laughs. "All you want to do is fuck her."

"Really, that's rich coming from you!" My voice rises with anger.

"What the fuck do you mean by that, huh?" Deacon takes another couple steps forwards. "You think that's all I want from her?"

"Yeah, I know that you do." I point to his journal. "Seems to me that that's the only thing you want from her. 'Everything about her screams take me...'" I quote his entry from journal. "That doesn't seem like someone who cares a whole lot about someone."

"You went through my shit!" Deacon starts to yell. "You trying to get me to kill you?"

"I'm looking for my friend, douchbag!" I shout.

Deacon roars and charges me, slamming me back into his desk. I wrap my arm around his head and try to force him down to the floor. But he's certainly stronger than me, even if I wasn't half dead. He lifts me up and throws me to the ground before diving on top of me. He wraps his hands around my throat and begins to strangle me.

"You know something?" he whispers, his voice straining with effort. "I've thought about doing this for a long fucking time." I begin to feel my strength leave my body as I struggle for air.

God, I'm so fucking sick of not being able to breathe!

Rage fills me, my vision going red as I lift my legs and lower body up, forcing Deacon off of me. He rolls onto the floor to my right, and I waste no time as I drive my knee into his stomach. He falls to the ground with a grunt as the air is knocked out of him. My fists begin to land recklessly and savagely against his face as I unleash all the pent-up rage I've been holding in since seeing my father die. I punch Deacon repeatedly, the wet thudding of my bloody, torn fists smacking into his face. The sounds of guttural grunting slowly fill my ears and I quickly realize it's me as I aggressively and hastily suck air in and out of my lungs.

The sick realization of what I'm doing takes over and my last punch lands on Deacon's face. I fall off him, taking a moment to look at my hands. The skin around my knuckles is shredded and bleeding heavily. Bone sticks out in some places. My eyes lock on to Deacon, who lies motionless on the floor beneath me. His face is caked in blood, both mine and his own. His eyes are swollen shut and his mouth agape. His nose is flat, definitely broken.

I start to panic. *I killed him! Oh, shit, I fucking killed him!*

I bend over, pressing my ear to his chest, hoping to hear a heartbeat. Seconds tick away and I start to freak out. Just as I'm about to give up, I hear the dull thud of Deacon's heartbeat. Followed slowly by another.

Oh, thank God!

I run my hands through my hair, relief flooding every part of my body. I look around the room, wondering what I should do next.

Should I call an ambulance? The bartender? Should I run and not look back?

I think for a bit on what I should be doing next. Before finally sitting down at Deacons desk. And there I sit, waiting. Praying.

And for the first time in my life, I pray that Deacon doesn't die.

***

I sit there for a little over three hours. The only thing I manage to do in that time is wash my hands in Deacon's bathroom. *Man, did that hurt.* My knuckles sting and throb like crazy, and I fear that they will most likely get infected. I check Deacon's pulse regularly and am continuously relieved to find it stable and growing stronger. Soon enough, I'm able to just watch his chest rise and fall as he breathes.

To kill time, I read more of his journal. Again, most of the entrances are about the bar and what he wants to do with it. His dream is to make is something nice and worth something, so he can sell it and try to buy a nightclub.

Of course, a nightclub. What else could a man ask for? Oh, I know...

The few entries not about the bar are about Zoë. Deacon seems to pride himself on how much he wants to get with her. He goes into great detail of what he would do with her. These things aren't worth repeating, but they are certainly never going to happen even if she ever decides to be with him.

Deacon begins to stir. He moans in pain and raises his hand to his eyes, rubbing away the dried blood from his face. His hand brushes past his nose and he shouts in pain.

"What the fuck?" he groans.

"I'm glad you're not dead." I snap close his journal and toss it onto his desk.

"What the fuck happened to me?" Deacon mumbles.

"I nearly killed you after you tried to kill me." I get up and walk over to Deacon, standing over him as he lays on the floor. "I want to say it felt good but honestly, I'm glad you're alive."

"Oh, fuck you." Deacon sits up. "You high and mighty cunt."

"Now that we've got that all out of the way and you aren't dead. We can talk about Zoë." I crouch down, meeting Deacon at eye level.

"Fuck," Deacon leans in closer to me, "you."

I nod my head, the familiar tingle of anger bubbles up in my throat. I stare at Deacon for a moment before bringing my arm back and slapping him hard across the face, sending him toppling to the floor once more.

"Ow, fuck!" he cries out.

"Listen to me, asshole!" I get on top of him, lifting him up by his shirt and getting in his face. "I have had the worst few weeks of my fucking life! Ok. You see my face." I turn my head, revealing the scarred half of my face, "That is just the fucking cherry on top of all the shit I've been through the past few weeks. So, I am fucking up to here with your wannabe tough guy act!" I drop him and stand up.

"Now I'm going to ask you one more time. And you are going to answer me. Otherwise," I raise my foot and place it on his chest. "I'll show you what it's like having the air ripped out of your lungs."

"Fuck man, ok! Just calm down!" Deacon begs.

"Calm down?" I ask.

Calm down. Calm down? I am so fucking sick of being calm!

I reach down and lift Deacon up off the floor by the collar of his shirt and push him against the liquor cabinet.

"I am fucking calm!" I scream in his face. He twists his face away from mine. "Now tell me where the fuck is Zoë!"

"Ok, ok!" Deacon cries out. "She's crashing at my cousin's place!"

"Your cousin's?"

"Yeah ok, shit I didn't know what else to do with her ok. Just please, let me go." I roll my eyes and drop Deacon, who falls pathetically to the floor.

"What the fucks she is doing at your cousin's place?"

"I don't know, ok?" Deacon groans. "She said she needed a place to crash for a few days, said she didn't wanna go home. I didn't have anywhere for her to stay at my place so I asked my cousin and he said I could let her crash there."

"Ok then," I lean down and pick Deacon up off the floor. "Looks like you and me are going for a ride. Hope you brought your car with you."

I shove Deacon to the door of his office, and together we head out of his office.

Chapter 12

We drive in silence. As we left the bar, the bartender, who I assumed was Cora, clearly saw Deacon and his injuries. He'd cleaned himself up a bit in the bathroom, but the swelling and bruising was hard to ignore. My mind raced as I tried to come up with an excuse before she gave me a quick wink and walked into the back room behind the bar.

Relieved, me and Deacon make our way to his car and head for his cousin's place. As we drive, I think about Zoë.

What will she think when I show up unannounced, with a beaten and bruised Deacon in tow? Will she be angry? Scared? Hell, maybe she might even like that I did something tough for once. God I'm such a hopeless fool.

We turn onto the street the Deacon says his cousin lives on. The area isn't very nice. Abandoned buildings sit all around this side of town. Not to mention the road, which was so poorly maintained it felt like Deacon's car would get stuck in a pothole. But we somehow make it to our destination. He pulls the car up and parks it on the side of the road just outside.

"This is it." Deacon mumbles. His face has swelled considerably, and, with his broken nose, speaking was hard for him.

"Ok, let's go then." I wait for Deacon to get out of the car first. Worried that he may try to ditch me.

We walk up to the front door and Deacon unlocks it. He pushes it open, looking to me as he does. Not caring for whatever it was he was about to say I push past him and step inside. The house is dark and dingy, with stale air disturbed only by our presence. We start to walk through the house; Deacon close behind me. But I see no sign of Zoë.

"Where is she?" I ask.

Deacon doesn't answer me. I turn around to repeat myself when I'm struck violently across the face by something blunt and heavy. I fall to the ground, my body already shutting down as I look up at a blurry Deacon. Stars begin to dance in my eyes and Deacon lifts what looks to be a bat.

"You should've just left it alone." He grunts as he brings the bat down on my head.

***

My feet sting as I walk forwards. The open sea stretches out before me, the setting sun leaves a crimson hue on the water's surface. The air smells and tastes of metal. I cry out as pain shoots up my right leg. I look down to see what happened and am stunned to see that I am not walking on a sandy beach.

The ground is made up entirely of black, shattered glass. Each shard smaller and sharper than the last. My feet bleed profusely from dozens of cuts and my right foot has a large shard of glass sticking up through its center. I lift it up and examine the glass. No, wrong again.

Obsidian. Of course, cause glass wasn't enough.

I touch the shard and lightning shoots through my leg.

I can't walk with this in my foot. I have no choice.

I grip the shard of obsidian tightly, its sharp edge immediately drawing blood from my hand. Gritting my teeth, I start to pull it out. The shard doesn't give at first, sending waves of pain shooting up through my leg. I strain with all my might and finally, the shard gives, sliding free from my foot.

I examine the obsidian for a moment. The shard is long and slender, almost a dagger in shape. It's edges so fine and sharp they could split and atom if I tried hard enough. My blood coats the shard, dripping lightly onto the ground. The setting sun glints off the blood, making appear as though it's glowing.

I look out at the sea before me, seeing it for what it truly is, an ocean of blood. The setting sun is almost engulfed by the horizon, and I fear for what will happen once it's gone. I walk a bit further, taking each step slowly in an attempt to avoid hurting my feet more than I already have, to no avail.

I reach the edge of the sea and crouch down, laying my left hand against the surface. The smell and taste of copper is overwhelming. I focus on the blood, picturing it becoming a sea of crystal-clear water. I think of the sun high in the sky, accompanied by a few gentle clouds. Finally, I think of the shattered glass that serves for a beach becoming a soft, lush field of grass.

My eyes open as I take a preemptive breath of fresh air. The ocean of blood greets me still. The sun has now dipped behind the horizon, its purple light fading into a black, starless night. The moon, however, is there, larger than I've ever seen it before. It was almost beautiful. If it wasn't so terrifying, that is.

Why didn't anything change?

What sounds like faint wind chimes ring out from behind me. I turn, carefully as to avoid hurting my feet, and am greeted by three tall, dark figures. They stand absolutely still, as though they're statues, but the whisps of shadows emanating around them reveal them to be something worse. They are dressed in short, black robes that glimmer like the obsidian sand we stand on.

But what's most shocking is their heads, which are much larger than that of normal humans and painted red. There were white symbols on their left cheeks that glowed, as though all the starlight in the sky was trapped within their faces. Their eyes were twice the size of mine, with small, red pupils. Finally, I looked to their mouths, which were twisted into a wicked smile that let show their long, curved teeth, almost tusks.

In unison, the figures all raise their hands into the air, as though they were holding baseball bats. Whisps of shadow curled up their arms, forming into long, sharp swords. They didn't move again. Nor did they speak or even breath. The air was still, the sounds of the sea of blood behind me being the only reprieve from what would be agonizing silence. The amulet, which still hung from my neck, began to burn. A faint hum emanating from it.

Demons? Really? Has the Dullahan run out of ideas to torment me with?

The first of the demons rushes forwards, jabbing its sword at me. I duck underneath the blade, rolling to the left. The shattered glass cuts me all over, each one equal to a bee sting. I try to stand but am forced to roll again as the demon continues to jap its sword at me. I fall to the ground, bleeding all over as tiny pieces of obsidian stick out of my skin. The second I stop moving, another demon appears behind me and slices its sword down at my head. I raise my hand to block it and feel the blade glide through it, severing it.

I scream in agony, instinctively kicking out at the demons' leg. I feel my toes break against it, and I seem to have done nothing to harm the demon. It raises its sword once more, hoping to deliver the killing blow. The loud snap of a whip tears through the air, and the demon freezes instantly.

"Every time we meet, I am thoroughly disappointed by your lack of imagination," the Dullahan chides.

I scramble to my feet, grabbing my severed hand off the ground as I turn and face the Dullahan. He looks the same, wearing a long trench coat, whisps of shadows coming off of him. His bald head in his left hand, his spine whip in his right. The wind gently flows around us. My shirt begins to burn as the amulet grows hotter.

"My lack of imagination?" I ask.

"Every time I've hunted a member of your family, they always try to fight me." The Dullahan holds up his head, facing me at eye level. I tense my body, preparing to look away at a moment's notice. "Usually, once they figure out that they can manipulate the world around us, they try to conjure weapons to fight me and the nightmares I've sent after them. They've tried everything. Guns, swords, mine fields. Your uncle even tried a nuclear bomb." The Dullahan smiles, "That one was quite entertaining."

"Yeah well, kinda hard to think about that kind of stuff when a demon is trying to cut your head off with a sword." I retort. "Besides, I tried to change where I am."

"Ah, yes, you like to do that I've noticed. It's a smart trick, changing the landscape of your nightmare makes it easy to run from it. However, this place," he holds up his arms, head and whip in both hands, gesturing to the air around us, "isn't my creation."

"It isn't?"

"No." he chuckles. "Finnan really has told you nothing, has he? That's quite a shame, you'd think he'd be more helpful preparing you to face me."

While the Dullahan talks, I slowly lift my severed hand and press it against the stump of my arm. A stinging pain shoots up my arm and it takes a lot to keep a straight face as the skin and bones glue themselves back together. The hum of the amulet grows louder and deeper, making my eyes vibrate in their sockets.

"He's done enough so far. Hell, if it wasn't for him, I would've been dead three times now." The wind gently billowing around us, sending a shiver down my spine.

"He has been annoyingly helpful in keeping you alive up to this point." He sighs. "But I suppose that was to be expected. He certainly doesn't want you to die yet."

"Yet?"

"What, did you think he was going to help stop me? Keep you alive so you can go through the rest of your life hopelessly chasing after a girl that doesn't want you?" the Dullahan mocks.

"Why wouldn't he help me, he's been doing enough so far. Three times now he's gotten in your way," I challenge.

"Five times actually," the Dullahan corrects. "But that was only for his benefit. After all if the pact is to continue, I do need to kill you."

"You mean the pact you made?"

"So, you know of the pact?" the Dullahan chuckles. "How interesting."

"Yeah, I know about it." I glare at him. "But I don't know why. I mean, what do you get out of all this? Why make a deal to wipe out my family?"

"I'm afraid I am not allowed to answer your questions." The Dulhan sighs. "You'd be better off asking Finnan."

"What does Finnan have to do with this?" I ask.

The Dullahan chuckles some more. "What did he tell you, hm? That this was done to him? That he's just another victim in a long line of dead men in your family?" The Dullahan starts to laugh, and the wind starts to pick up around him. "Yes, he does like to play innocent in all this."

"Are you saying this is Finnan's fault?"

"The fact you don't already know shows how poor of a job he's done preparing you to face me." The Dullahan raises his voice, the wind hollowing around us as he does.

"Why would he do this to his own family?" I holler over the wind. "Why are you killing my family?"

I look behind me for a moment. The demon hasn't moved an inch. Its sword held high in the air, ready to deliver the killing blow. I look back to the Dullahan.

"I mean the last time we spoke, in the dessert. I got the impression that you didn't like doing this. Hunting me and my family for generations."

"I don't, at least not anymore."

"Then why do you do it?"

"Because that was the price Finnan must pay for power." The wind rips through the air, stinging my skin. The amulet is so hot now I fear it will melt a hole through my chest.

"What price? What deal did you make with Finnan?" I shout.

"It doesn't matter anymore. It cannot be undone by either of us. But it will soon be over," His voice is calm and flows over the wind as though it wasn't there. "And I'll be free."

The Dullahan's eyes open. I leap backwards, twisting my body as I do so to avoid looking him in the eyes. I cover my face with my arms as I dive into the glass. I feel intense heat flow over my back for only a moment, before vanishing as soon as it had appeared. My back however, stung as though I'd just been given a sunburn.

He closed his eyes!

I take this as my chance, lifting myself up and start to run for the bloody sea. A searing pain rips through my stomach, and I look down to see the end of a sword sticking through me. I look up behind me to see the face of the demon starring down at me with a gleeful madness.

'My lack of imagination?'

I picture the glass beneath the demons' feet. Rather than it changing into something else, I simply picture more of it. I picture it bottomless, like quicksand. Sucking in anything unfortunate enough to step on it. Almost instantly, the demon sinks up to its knees in the glass. It doesn't look away from me, holding onto the sword that sticks though me.

I feel the sword inside me, and I picture it getting hot. White hot. So hot that it begins to melt and split in half from the weight of the demon as it sinks ever more into the glass. As so it does. The heat is almost unbearable as the sword begins to radiate heat, boiling my blood from the inside. Whilst on the outside it begins to bend and stretch, making it so the demon sinks deeper into the glass. With a sickening pop, the blade breaks in half and the demon falls into an endless abyss of glass and darkness.

I'm about to celebrate when I hear the cracking of a whip. I turn in time to see the whip slam into me. At least, it should've. The whip collides with the amulet on my chest and an explosion of golden light fills the space between me and the Dullahan. I remain unscathed while the Dullahan screams in fury and pain. I look at him to see what could have hurt him.

His whip has turned into gold. Instantly he drops it, his hand igniting into a golden flame. He howls with fury and the two remaining demons begin to charge me. Acting purely on reflex I flick my arm and a wall of obsidian erupts from the ground between us. Taking to more time to watch, I turn and run, just a few feet away from the sea of blood.

The Dullahan screams in fury, his now golden whip wrapping itself around my leg, pulling me to the ground. I look back once more to see the whip, alight with a golden flame, held fiercely and painfully by the Dullahan. The whip clings to me tightly, but unlike ever before, I feel no pain.

My hands move on their own, as if being controlled by someone. I rip the amulet off the cord around my neck and feel it melt and reform in my palm. Withing seconds, the amulet is now a golden dagger. Seeing what I need to do, I cut the whip, sending the Dullahan ablaze as he is engulfed completely in golden fire. His howls of pain and fury shake the world around me as I scramble to my feet.

I look at the ocean of blood and get a crazy idea. I picture the sea like I pictured the glass. Not changing, but endless. I think of the intense winds brought by the Dullahan, and I imagine them lifting the sea up into a massive tsunami.

The two remaining demons cut through the wall of obsidian and begin to rush towards me. The sea begins to heave and turn, the wind gaining direction as it carries the blood towards the glassy shore. And with a definitive roar from the Dullahan, the sea erupts.

A tsunami of blood lifts itself high into the air. Were there any stars I'd say it would be touching them. As fast as the wave of blood rose, to fell right on top of the

Dullahan and me, carrying us both away in is warm, salty depths.

***

The sea of blood is thick and hot. Whereas in the ocean before I was able to open my eyes, this time the blood burns my eyes with a fury. The current heaves and pulls me in every direction all at once. Through the blood, the howling of wind can still be heard, though muted. And through it all, the snapping of a whip. Although my eyes are shut tight and I am buried under a sea of blood, with each crack of the Dullahan's whip, light flashes across my eyes.

I started trying to swim, letting the current help lead me away from the Dullahan. I swim for as long as I could, my lungs being crushed by the lack of air. The current disappears as what little strength I had in my body runs dry. I fear I'm about to die.

Just like Dad, drowning.

Grim determination fills me.

I will not die like this!

I picture a whirlpool. I see the bloody sea ripped apart as wind rips through it from two directions. Down to the very bottom, where I pray is solid ground and not more broken obsidian. For a moment, nothing happens. My lungs are about to burst when the roaring of the blood being thrown about by the wind explodes all around me. The blood around me is violently ripped away and warm, foul smelling air rushes down my throat.

The whirlpool grows wider and deeper. Reaching down further than I previously expected, until finally the bottom of the sea is revealed. The current from the whirlpool slowly sucks me down until at least I reach the bottom. My legs give out from under me and I collapse onto the solid, white ground. I rest for a few moments, thankful for solid ground.

How can Finnan like sailing when solid ground is so lovely?

I take a deep breath and sit up, taking a moment to examine my wounds. All over, my body is covered in thin, deep cuts. My foot aches from my broken toes and where I'd pulled the shar of obsidian out of it. My stomach also bleeds heavily from where the demon stabbed me, part of its sword still sticking out just above my belly button.

I grip the blade and scream in anguish as I pull it from my stomach. Dark blood oozes from the wound and spots dance in my vision. I take several long, deep breaths. Trying to focus on making my wounds heal. As usual, it takes a few seconds to start working, but work it does. I feel the cuts all over my body stitch back together, my toes snapping back into place, and the hole than runs through my core shrink and close in on itself. My foot falls asleep as it closes the hole in its center. Before you know it, I'm back in fighting shape.

I look up at the sky above me, the large moon stares down at me like the Eye of Sauron. I sigh and go to stand up but stop and stare at the floor I rest on. The ground shines white in the moonlight, its surface smooth and glossy. Almost like a waxed bone. I shiver at the thought and push myself up, taking a moment to test my leg. I look to my right hand and find the amulet, restored to its image, gripped tightly within it.

Where were you all this time, huh?

When I fail to collapse, I know I'm ready. I look forwards at the spinning wall of blood that encircles me. My eyes tracking its surface up to where it meets the sky.

The ocean is deeper than the tallest mountain I can imagine.

This world would be pretty cool to explore if I constantly wasn't about to die.

I look down at the bone I stand on and imagine it rising as the sea of blood forces its way underneath it. The ground starts to groan and rumble when I do.

That's the trick. I can't manipulate the form the world takes, only what happens to it. I was able to change the forest into an ocean before because the forest was a nightmare created by the Dullahan to trap me. But the ocean of blood and the beach of broken obsidian were already here in this world when the Dullahan and I came here. I can't change that, no more than you can change the pieces on a game board. I can, however, change where the pieces are.

The bone floor shakes violently as it is dislodged from the sea, and it begins to rise to the surface. The sound of the blood rushing under the bone is more akin to paint being poured into a bucket than water. As I ride the bone up, the walls of the blood ocean seem to form a tunnel to the sky. I look up at the moon, which seems to grow brighter the closer I get to it. Just before I reach the surface of the ocean, the white light from the moon engulfs me. And everything fades away...

Chapter 13

My eyes open and are greeted with darkness. I take a quick breath and the damp smell of a basement fills my nose. I try to get up off the floor but find it difficult as my arms and legs are zip-tied. I look around the room to try and find something to help me but find nothing.

I tug at the zip-ties for a while, ripping the skin around my wrists raw. While I fumble with them, I think about everything that's happened: *So, Finnan made a pact with the Dullahan? Was the Dullahan lying to me? Or did Finnan really make everything up?*

The only way to be certain is to confront Finnan. If he was lying, if the Dullahan was telling the truth, then his reaction will show it. But first, I have to find Zoë.

The zip-tie finally snaps, and my hands are freed. My wrists hurt but I don't feel any blood so I'm sure I'm ok. I start to tug at the zip-ties around my feet and soon they come free as well.

But what about Zoë? Clearly this isn't where Deacon was hiding her. Is she still in trouble? Where is Deacon? Why am I still alive?

So many questions racing through my head as I sit in this cold, dark basement. The ground is solid stone, and it sucks whatever warmth I had out of my body. I stand up and immediately pull my phone out of my pocket. I'm about to call the police when I see that I have no service.

God dammit, the one time I actually need this piece of shit to work!

My head hanging, I decide to inspect the walls, hoping to find a light switch. After a bit of searching, I find a cord hanging from the ceiling. I tug it and a single, small light clicks to life.

With the room now illuminated, I take a careful look around. The basement is completely empty, with half painted walls and no way out other than a single staircase.

Deciding I had no other choice, I quietly make my way up the stairs. Cautiously stepping on the edges of the steps as to not make any noise. When I reach the door, I slowly try opening it. Unsurprisingly, its locked.

That motherfucker!

I make my way back down the stairs and start to scour every inch of the room. As I search the room, I think about what the Dullahan said to me.

What could Finnan have to gain from making a deal with the Dullahan? He's dead as far as I'm aware, so what? Did he really become king? Did he even have a wife?

All the questions repeat themselves over and over again in my head, driving me mad.

I'm just about to give up on searching the basement when my eyes lock onto a wall outlet. I stare at it for a long time and start to formulate a plan around it. I make my way back up the stairs and inspect the door. The lock is a more modern one, just a small little hole in the handle.

If I can get some of the wire from the wall outlet, I can jimmy the lock and open the door!

I race back down the stairs and begin to rip apart the outlet. At first, I struggle because it's screwed into the wall. The wall is drywall, so I decide that my only option is to rip it apart. I'm about to punch the wall just to the left of the outlet when I see my mangled hands.

Not only are they heavily scarred from the nails in the cross, but they also are swelled and scabbed over around my knuckles. The scabs are a dark green color, and I know for a fact they are infected. I grit my teeth and with a grimace, punch the wall. The wall gives slightly, but not enough. My hand throbs as I punch the wall again. The wall cracks around the outlet, giving me hope that my plan will work. With a final punch the wall breaks and after stifling a moan of pain, I'm able to rip the wall apart. I peel the wall away around the outlet and reach behind the outlet, grabbing a handful of wires.

I rip them loose and start to pull a short, thin piece of copper wire free. I race swiftly back up the steps and fumble with the lock for a minute and hear a dull click as the lock releases. My hand shakes as I reach for the handle and slowly turn it, opening the door. I step out into the hallway and am relieved to find the house dark and quiet.

Deacon isn't here.

I race to the front door and step outside. I'm still in the house where Deacon attacked me before. The sky is dark, and light rain falls from the sky. The greater city just off in the distance shines seductively, as if luring me away from the run-down shithole neighborhood I currently stand in. I take no time to celebrate as I race off down the road.

I'm coming for you, Deacon!

***

I barge in the front door of Deacon's bar and make my way up to the bartender. It's the same girl from before.

"Cora, right?" I ask her.

"Yep," she turns to look at me and is shocked to see me. "Oh, hey, you're the kid from earlier."

"Yeah, Deacon ditched me out on the east side. I need to find him."

"Look, kid, whatever you and him got going on, I don't want any part of." She goes to walk away.

"Look just, please," I plead. "I'm looking for my friend, that girl you saw me with before, Zoë. I think she's in trouble and Deacon knows where she is."

"Look kid I-"

"Please, I need your help!" I cut her off.

She looks at me for a moment. A patron at the counter leans over towards us.

"Hey, sweetie, mind if I get another beer?" He slurs his words. He looks at me. "You need something, kid?"

I ignore him. "Please, Cora I need to find him."

"Hey, I'm talkin' to you, kid." The guy pokes my shoulder.

"Look, I can go try to call him, but that's it, ok?" Cora goes to the phone behind her.

"Hey, is someone going to pay attention to me?" the patron shouts.

"Look man, we're busy right now, just give us a couple minutes," I bark at him.

"Whoa, tuff little man, huh?" The patron stands up. "You got something to prove, kid? Maybe trying to impress the lady huh?"

"What's your problem, man?"

Another patron speaks up. "Frank, leave the kid alone."

The man whose name is Frank looks to the friendly patron and tells at him to mind his own business. He looks back to me and takes a step closer to me. I can smell alcohol on his breath.

"You wanna talk to me now, kid?"

Cora gets off the phone and turns back around. "Frank!" she slams a beer on the counter. "Here's your beer, sit down, now!"

"Not till this little punk says sorry," Frank snarls.

"Sorry? For what?" I ask.

"Being disrespectful," Frank answers. "When someone speaks to you, you answer him. Now, apologize!"

"Look, whatever man." I go to talk to Cora, my blood boiling.

"I said apologize!" Frank shoves me.

Without thinking, I grab the bottle of beer off the counter and smash it over the side of Frank's head. He stumbles to the side a bit, dazed. Without hesitation, I kick him in the knee as hard as I can. His leg bends the wrong way and Frank collapses under his own weight. The bar, which is half full, goes silent and stares in disbelief as Frank begins to cry out in pain. I look back to Cora.

"Do you know where Deacon is?" I demand.

Cora is silent for a moment, in shock at what she just saw. To snap her out of it, I pound the table with my fist, sending a jolt of pain up my arm.

"Cora!" I shout.

"Jesus!" she shouts. "He said he was at a club. I don't know where though."

Purgatory.

"Thanks." I turn and am about to walk away. I stop as I look down at Frank. He's crying and clutching his leg. The bar is dead silent except for his sobbing. Everyone inside looks at me.

Two weeks ago, I'd never have even thought of doing something like that to someone. I'd only ever been in a couple fights back in middle school and high school.

Now, I've beaten someone within an inch of their life and shattered another man's knee. I must be going crazy.

With a stone in my stomach, I walk out the front of Deacon's bar and make my way toward Purgatory.

***

I push open the secret door that leads to Purgatory and slowly make my way down the steps. My heart pounds in my chest like a cannon being fired. My throat is dry, and my legs hurt. I arrive in the front room to the club and am greeted by a bouncer.

"Can I help you?" He looks me up and down. I must look like a psychopath.

"Beautiful day, huh?" I ask.

"Indeed," the bouncer nods. "Could use some rain though."

"To wash away the sins of man." I answer.

The bouncer shakes his head. "Sorry kid, wrong answer."

"What do you mean? I was just here a couple weeks ago, that was it."

"Yeah, a couple weeks ago that was it. It changes every week. Members get a message letting them know what the phrase is to prevent guests from coming and going as they please."

"Come on, man," I beg. "I need to get in there. I won't even be an hour; I just need to find someone."

"Who do you need to find?" the bouncer asks. "I can leave them a message telling them you were here."

"Look, I don't even know if they're here. I just need to look around the place. Please man, you can't just let this slide?"

He shakes his head. "Sorry, kid. Even if I wanted to, cameras wouldn't let that fly." He points to a small camera behind him, hiding in the corner.

"Then what do I have to do to get you to let me in?"

"You could become a member."

"How much will that cost me?"

"300 bucks a month."

"300 bucks!" I shout.

"That or you can wait for your friend outside," the bouncer says.

I can't wait outside; I don't even know if Deacon is here. But I don't have any money either.

"I don't have that much."

"Then you won't get in." The bouncer picks up his phone off the desk and starts to scroll through it.

Defeated, I make my way back up the stairs. As I step outside, the rain starting to pour down on me, I try to look for a spot to sit and wait.

I don't have any other choice.

***

I wait for nearly two hours. My clothes are soaked to the bone from the endless rain. My body is wracked and beaten. Exhaustion eats away at me. On the upside, it's so cold and wet outside that no matter how tired I am, I won't be able to fall asleep.

The hidden door to Purgatory has opened a couple times throughout my stakeout with people coming and going. Each time I'm disappointed as Deacon is not one of those who exit the club.

Again, I never thought I'd be seeking out Deacon so aggressively. Normally I try to avoid the snake. But I need to find Zoë.

The door to Purgatory opens and a single man exits the club. I quickly get up from my pile of trash that I hide in and start to follow him. Just before we reach the street, the man's phone rings, and he answers it.

"Hello?" My heart jumps with joy as I hear Deacon's voice. His speech is still messed up as a result of his nose.

Good.

"Wait, what?" Deacon speaks up. "He did what!" he shouts. "Ok, ok listen. Shut up for a second and listen. I'll handle that punk ok, just leave it alone. I'll talk to Frank, too, make sure he won't sue." He pauses as the person on the other end of the phone speaks. "Cora, just lock up the bar and go home, ok? Take tomorrow off and think about this before you do anything rash, ok? I've got to go." He hangs up the phone. "That motherfucker!" he shouts.

That call was about Frank. Seems Cora didn't appreciate someone doing something about those scumbags she deals with at that shithole bar.

Deacon makes his way down the street, and I follow behind him. The street is mostly empty, so I keep my distance. At one point Deacon looks back at me and I turn down an alleyway while he watches. I wait awhile and when I emerge, he's farther down the road.

Finally, after walking for about ten minutes, I see Deacon's car.

Shit! I can't follow him in a car!

Just a dozen feet away from his car, he reaches into his pocket and pulls out his keys, unlocking it. It's then that a man appears in front of Deacon, stopping him. The man starts to talk to him. I overhear Deacon shout at him to go away. The man doesn't and instead starts to beg for Deacon to buy his mixtape. While Deacon is distracted, I make my way over and hide behind his car, making sure he cannot see me.

Swiftly, I open the truck and slip inside, making sure to put my shirt sleeve in the lock of the door so to not lock myself inside. While in his car, I hear Deacon telling the man off for the third time. Defeated, the man finally leaves Deacon alone. Deacon's footsteps thud like the hooves of the Dullahan's horses as he reaches his car and slips inside. The engine starts and the car takes off.

I'm coming, Zoë!

***

As we drive, Deacon listens to some punk rock. As if the drive wasn't bad enough being jammed in his trunk, but Deacon decides to sing along with the music. We drive along like this for about a half hour until finally Deacon comes to a stop. I hear him open and slam his car door and start to walk away.

Hastily I push open the trunk door and almost fall out of his car. I get back up, making sure to close the trunk just in case and start after Deacon. We're in a small car park in a slightly nicer part of town than the house he led me to before. Deacon makes his way towards a set of elevators. I follow closely behind him, being as careful as possible to not draw any attention to myself. When he reaches the elevator, he steps inside, and the doors close behind him.

Dammit, it's never this hard in movies!

I stand in front of the elevator for a few minutes as I watch the floor number tick up. At last, it stops on floor number fourteen. I call the elevator back and follow suit. As I wait in the elevator, my hard won't stop beating. My hands shake and sweat stings my eyes.

This is it. I need to find whatever room Deacon is staying in and pray that Zoë is with him!

The elevator doors ding and open, revealing a narrow hallway. I start to panic at first. So many rooms and I have no idea where to begin. Deciding I have no other choice, I start knocking on doors.

The first couple doors I knock on nothing happens. The third, an older woman answers the door. I speak to her for a few moments, asking her if she's seen Deacon or Zoë around and she tells me she hasn't. I thank her for her time and move on.

The fourth door doesn't open, but a deep voiced man speaks to me through it, telling me to fuck off. I try asking for his help, but he cuts me off saying he isn't interested in anything I have to say. Not wanting to push my luck, I move on to the next door.

This time, the door opens revealing a large man dressed in construction gear. His big, with dark skin and a mean mug. He looks me up and down, taking in my disheveled appearance before asking me what I want.

"Sorry to bother you, sir," I tell him, "But I was hoping you could help me find a couple of people."

"What for?"

"You see," *Here we go!* "I'm trying to catch my girlfriend cheating."

"Your girlfriend?" the man raises an eyebrow in confusion.

"Yes. I think she's cheating on me. I followed her here, but I don't know what room she's in right now. Even if I somehow found the room she's staying in, the guy she's with might turn me away, so I was hoping you could help me find the room the guy is staying in and then I could catch them together." I lie like never before. My heart bounces off my ribcage as I pull all this out of my ass.

"You know the guy she's cheating on you with?" the man asks.

"Deacon Winters," I tell him.

The guy nods his head. "Yeah, I know Deacon, but do you?"

"Um, tall guy. Skinny, with slicked back hair and a beard, sometimes stubble. Has a faded, red leather jacket."

"Mhm." The guy nods his head some more. "And your girl, got any proof she exists?"

"Yes, yes I do!" I scramble and grab my phone out of my pocket. I turn it on and show the guy my home screen. It's a picture of Zoë and I at the aquarium. A happy beluga whale smiles at us in the background.

The man looks at the photo for a long time. Taking in every detail. Soon, he hands it back to me.

"I've seen her around," he says.

"You have? When?" I ask, putting all my acting talent into the lie.

"A couple days ago," he answers. "She was pretty messed up. I think her and that guy she's with are on something."

"I knew it!" *He's buying it! Thank God!*

"Just tell me one thing." He holds up his hand. "What's her name?"

"Zoë St. John."

The guy looks at me for a few moments as he makes up his mind about whether to believe me or not.

"Look, I know this seems super sketchy. If you wanna call the cops, I completely understand. I won't resist. But I'm telling you the truth. If she's cheating on me, I need to see for myself." I pray he doesn't call my bluff.

The guy sighs deeply. "Ok. She's in that apartment down there." He points at the door on the far-right end of the hallway. "But just so we are clear, I'm going to take a picture of you. So, in case something happens, I can give it to the police."

"Absolutely. I understand."

He pulls out his phone and takes a quick picture of me. "Ok then, one last thing. What's your name?"

"Aaron Ward."

"Ok Aaron Ward." The man sighs. "I don't feel too good about this but I'm being nice right now because I need to get to work. I hope what you've told me is the truth. And I wish you luck."

"Thank you, sir." I shake his hand. "I promise you; nothing is going to happen. I just need to talk with her. That's it."

"Ok, go." I start off down the hallway. Halfway down it, the man shouts at me and I stop to look back at him. "I better not ever see you here again, Aaron Ward. Cause if I do, the police will be the last of your problems." With that, the man opens the elevator and steps inside. The doors close behind him, and he vanishes.

Thank you, dude! You have no idea how much you just helped me!

Chapter 14

I stare at the door to Deacon's apartment. My heart pounds in my throat as my hands shake and sweat profusely. I'm nervous beyond belief. Who wouldn't be? As worried for Zoë as I am, I don't know if she is actually in danger. From the sound of things, she might be here of her own free will. If that's the case, she might not appreciate me barging in on her. Let alone what I did to Deacon.

"Fuck it," I whisper and knock on the door.

I make sure to cover the peephole as I wait for Deacon or Zoë to come to the door. After a few seconds, I hear Deacon's voice shushing on the other side of the door. *Keeping Zoë quiet.*

"Who is it?" Deacon asks. "Why are you covering the peephole?"

"I'm not." I make my voice sound deeper to try and throw him off. "I'm with the Chicago Police Department and I would just like to ask you some questions."

"About what?" Deacon asks.

Damn, I'm a better liar than I thought.

"I'm investigating a missing persons case," I answer, my voice straining as I try to mask it, "a Zoë St. John."

"Don't know who that is. Seriously why are you covering the peephole?" Deacon challenges.

"Sir, I can assure you I'm not covering the peephole." I cough, my throat starting to hurt. "Is this Deacon Winters I'm speaking with?"

"This is Deacon. I don't have a clue where Zoë is."

He sounds nervous. Good.

"Sir, I promise you, you aren't in any trouble. Is there any way you'd be willing to step outside so I can ask you a few questions please?" My voice cracks halfway through the sentence and I cross my finger, hoping Deacon doesn't notice.

"You got a warrant?" he asks.

"No, sir." I answer, annoyed. "That's why I'm asking you to step outside. I promise you aren't being charged with anything. We just need to ask a few questions."

"Fine. I'm coming out," Deacon sighs.

I keep my fingers on the peephole. My body tenses up as I prepare to barge into the room. The door unlocks and I hear Deacon turn the handle. The instant the door starts to open I throw myself at it, sending Deacon flying backwards into the apartment. I enter and quickly slam the door behind me. Deacon pushes himself off the floor, furious.

"Ward!" he shouts. "What the fuck?"

I brace myself for a fight as Deacon gets ready to attack me. Just before he dives at me, we freeze at the sound of Zoë's voice:

"What's happening over there?" she shouts.

"Zoë!" I shout. "It's me, Aaron!"

"Aaron?" I hear the running footsteps and Zoë suddenly appears around the corner of the short hallway. "What the hell are you doing here?"

"I'm here for you." I answer back, relieved to see her looking unharmed. "What the hell are you doing here?"

"What am I doing here?" she says, taken aback.

"Your dad is worried sick!" I push passed Deacon, who struggles to let me past. "No one has heard from you in a week. I was worried."

She rolls her eyes and walks back into the living room of the apartment. I follow, acutely aware of Deacon behind me.

"So what? I needed a little me time. Is that such a big deal?" Zoë asks.

"It is when you don't tell anyone anything. Your dad even called the police and filed a missing person's report."

"God, he's so over dramatic." She flops down on the couch in the center of the room.

The apartment is nice and roomy. With a large L-shaped couch in the center of the room facing the T.V. between two large windows. Behind the couch is a small kitchen, with a few boxes of pizza resting on the countertops. In front of the couch is a glass coffee table. No wonder Deacon's struggling with money. He lives like a bachelor with daddy's trust fund.

"Zoë, you've had everyone worried." I emphasize everyone.

"Everyone. Who? My dad? You? Who else, huh?" she argues. "Who else cares that I took a week off from everyone's bullshit?"

"Zoë, please just-"

She cuts me off. "No, Aaron! How about I ask you what you are doing here, hm?" she shouts. "Kicking in Deacon's door after beating the crap out of him earlier. How did you even find me? Did you follow us?"

"Yes but-"

"No, no buts!" she shouts. "You look like shit; you've attacked my friend and now you just expect me to be happy you're here?"

The room goes silent as Zoë and I stare at each other. I'm speechless, she's right. She's totally right. *Except…*

"So, you just needed some you time." I say, calmly. "I get that. But I don't understand why you didn't tell me or your dad. You weren't answering your phone, you didn't tell anyone what you were doing. How long you'd be gone. Nothing. You just expected us to not worry?"

"That's not what I'm saying," she says.

"Then what are you saying?" I shout at her. "Christ Zoë! I don't get you. First you tell you don't love me. Fine, I get that. Then you disappear for a week. Ok, I can understand you need some time to yourself. But you didn't tell anyone, anything! And now I get the shit beaten out of me by your creepy friend over there," I point at Deacon, who has moved into the kitchen, "and then get tied up in his fucking basement! All while trying to find you by the way. And you're mad at me for giving a shit?"

Zoë is silent as she takes in everything I've said. She looks to Deacon, who glares at me.

"You tied him up?" she asks, her tone ice cold.

He looks at her and stifles a laugh. "Oh what, you believe this asshole?"

"Oh, give me a break!" I shout at him. "I went to your shitty bar looking for Zoë and you attacked me. You tried to kill me, so I beat the fuck out of you." I turn back to Zoë, "Afterwards I made him take me to where he said you were staying. When we got to the house, he said you were crashing at he knocked me out and tied me up in his basement."

"Deacon!" Zoë yells at him. "What the fuck?"

"The little shit broke into my office! Was going through my all my shit!" he yells back at her.

"So, you kidnapped him?"

"No!" he studders. "Yes, but it isn't like that. The guy was trying to take you away from me."

"Take me away from you?" Zoë echoes.

"Yes! I didn't want you to go with him."

"I'm not yours to take away!" She looks at me, "Neither of you!"

"You're seriously still mad at me?" I ask her.

"I don't know what to think!" she shouts. "This is insane!"

"Look," Deacon holds up his hands in a peaceful gesture. "I get that you're mad right now. But this guy," he points at me, "is fucking crazy. First you get into a fight with a bouncer at the club, then you lash out at Zoë. Talking about how much you love her or whatever. Then you disappear from her." He lowers his hands. "She didn't get any texts or calls from you. You didn't care. Now you're trying to convince her that I'm the bad guy here?"

"Ok, both of you just shut up!" Zoë shouts.

The room is dead silent as she thinks for a moment. Me and Deacon glare at each other.

"Aaron. Why didn't you call or text me?" she asks.

"I didn't think you wanted me, too!" I answer. "I figured after the hospital you wanted to be left alone. If it wasn't for the fact you disappeared for a week, I wouldn't have bothered you. But I got worried."

She holds up her hand, silencing me. "Enough." She thinks for another moment. She looks to Deacon, "Why did you attack Aaron? You knew he was worried about me, so why did you attack him. Then tied him up in…," she looks back at me, "I'm sorry. A basement?"

"He said it was his cousin's place. Told me you were staying there, that's how he got the jump on me." I clarify.

"Right." She looks back at Deacon. "Care to explain?"

Deacon opens his mouth, but no words come out. I fight the urge to smile.

"So, nothing?" Zoë asks. "Ok." She gets up off the couch and makes her way to what I assume is the bedroom.

"Hey, wait, what are you doing?" Deacon chases after her.

"I'm leaving." Zoë answers. "He may be annoying right now but at least he isn't nuts like you."

"Zoë come on, don't do this." Deacon grabs her arm as she goes to leave.

"Hey!" I push him away. "Don't touch her."

Deacon frowns and pulls out a gun from his waistband.

"What now, motherfucker?!" he shouts at me.

"Jesus! Deacon, put that away!" Zoë yells.

"Shut up!" he shouts at her. "Everything I've done for you. All the shit I did for you and this," he looks me up and down, "this fucker is what takes you away from me."

"Deacon, please. Put that down," Zoë begs.

Stay calm. Just stay calm. Wait for an opportunity.

"No. No, no, no. No, after all this bullshit, I'm not gonna let this little shit walk away thinking he's won." He looks at her, "And I sure as shit ain't letting you leave me now."

Now!

I slap the gun in Deacon's hand away and he pulls the trigger. I throw myself into him, tackling him to the floor. I wrestle him the floor and try to rip the gun away from him. He starts to claw at my face with his free hand and I bite his thumb off. He screams out in pain and the gun goes off a couple more times. Deacon lifts himself up and throws me off him. He goes to shoot me and I kick him in the chest. The gun goes off again and I feel a bullet rip through my arm.

Adrenaline courses through my veins making it so any pain I'd normally feel is ignored. I scramble back up on my feet. My eyes lock onto Deacon as he points the gun at me and pulls the trigger, with a sharp click, the gun doesn't fire

Out of bullets motherfucker!

Deacon drops the gun to the ground and charges me. His head slams into my chest and I feel my feet lift off the floor as Deacon rams me into the door of his apartment. I feel the door give slightly under the force of our impact as I push Deacon away. He instantly uppercuts me, and I feel my head start to spin.

I slump forwards, dazed, and Deacon decides to finish me off with a definitive kick to the chest. I careen back into his door once more. And once more I feel it give under the force, only this time a little more than before. I fall to the ground, my arms limp at my sides. And I look up through at Deacon through cloudy vision.

"You just couldn't leave well enough alone, could you?" He taunts.

I cough as I begin to stand up, slowly drawing air into my lungs.

"Now, I'm gonna show you what happens when you fuck with me." He brings his leg back, preparing to kick me.

I scream and throw myself at him, pushing him back into the apartment. But he's stronger than me, I have nothing left to give. And he screams along with me as he forces me back into the door one final time. The door gives way under the combined weight and force of us, being ripped off of its hinges.

Deacon and I stumble over the destroyed door and land in the hallway of the building. Deacon propped himself up over me and began to beat me. Over and over again without a shred of restraint and understanding of what he was doing. I fear I am about to be knocked out, my head buzzes with a cold numb feeling radiating all around me. Then, the punching stops.

I faintly hear Deacon and someone else yelling and fighting with each other. The lights in the hallway shine down on me, but my eyes are already swelling shut. I groan and roll onto my side. The commotion from Deacon and someone else comes to an end and I look over at them, barley able to see what was happening.

It was the neighbor from before. He stood over an unconscious Deacon, his foot resting on Deacons back. He looks to me and shock spreads across his face.

"Holy shit kid! You sure know how to take a beating," I smile weakly at him.

I look away as he starts to say something else, but I'm not listening.

Where is Zoë?

I make my way back into Deacon's apartment, stumbling over the destroyed door. Once inside, I hear sobbing. I walk into the living room and see Zoë lying on the floor. Blood pooling around her from a hole in her stomach. A final burst of adrenaline tears through me and I rush to her side. I press my mangled hands together over her stomach, trying desperately to stop the bleeding.

"Zoë, Zoë it's gonna be ok. I promise. Just look at me ok."

Through a stream of tears, she looks up at me, eyes wide with fear, "Aaron, I don't wanna die."

"You're not dying, ok? Just look at me, it's going to be ok. I'm right here." I look around for something to use and see her things.

A bag of clothes and her phone sits just in front of the hallway that leads to the front door. I reach over and grab the bag, tearing it open with one hand as the other tries to stop the bleeding. I pull out a T-shirt and roll it up.

"Here, take this." I press the T-shirt against her stomach. I take her hands and fold them over it. "Put pressure right here, ok? Don't move, ok?"

She nods at me.

I hear Deacon's neighbor walk in behind me and he gasps in shock.

"What the hell happened?"

I turn to face him, "Call an ambulance!"

He pulls his phone out of his pocket and starts to dial. While he does, I look back to Zoë.

"Hey, hey it's ok. I'm right here. The ambulance is on its way, ok. You're going to be fine."

"Aaron. I'm sor-" She starts to say.

"No, none of that, ok. Just look at me, ok. It's all ok, just stay here with me. You're hear with me. Just, don't fall asleep." I urge her.

We stay there for a few minutes. I hear sirens ringing out. I start to feel light-headed as my heart rate slows. I'd gotten so used to being in a constant state of panic. The room is absolutely quiet as I keep my hands pressed against Zoë's stomach. I look over at neighbor as he makes his way out of the apartment.

Where are you going?

I look back to Zoë to see that her eyes have closed.

"Zoë?" I shake her and she doesn't respond. "Zoë!" I press my ear against her chest and try to listen for her heartbeat. After 10 seconds, I hear nothing.

Panicking, I get on my knees over her, pressing my hands together over her chest. I start to perform CPR. I hear her ribs cracking underneath the pressure as I do so. I reach down and press my lips to hers, forcing air down her throat. I do this about eight or nine times.

"Zoë, please," I beg, tears welling in my eyes. "Please don't do this to me, please."

I'm still performing CPR when police rush into the apartment, followed closely by the paramedics. The police pull me off Zoë as the paramedics start to work on her. They take an oxygen mask out and lay it over her face. Afterwards they lift her up onto a gurney and wheel her away. The police don't let me go with her.

***

I'm sitting in an interrogation room at the police station. My hands and arm are bandaged and cuffed to the table. A

Styrofoam cup of water rests in my hands. The doctor had made a comment on how brutally scarred my hands were. I didn't speak to him. I haven't made a sound since they took Zoë away.

My hands throb but I don't feel any pain. The doctor gave me some aspirin. He also took a look at my arm. Thankfully, the bullet had only grazed me. He stitched me up and then I was sent to wait here. They'd taken my amulet away from me first. Not having it around my neck made me feel vulnerable.

Please. Please be ok. I don't know what I'd do if you died.

The door opens and in walk a pair of men. They are very different from each other. The first one is wearing a simple brown suit. He's tall, with balding brown hair, and a clean-shaven face. His eyes are bright blue, and they stare right through me.

The second man is younger. He is wearing a simple black button-up with the sleeves rolled up. He's a bit shorter than the first guy, with a shaggy head of sandy, blond hair. He has a short goatee with some stubble. Both have badges hanging from their necks.

Detectives. Great.

They both sit down across from me.

"Hello, Aaron," the tall one says, his voice deep. "I'm Detective Joseph Griffin and this is my partner, Detective Fisher."

"Hello." Fisher's voice is monotone. He's not interested in talking, I guess.

I say nothing to either of them.

"Now, Aaron. May I call you Aaron?"

Again, I don't reply.

"You see, Aaron, we have a few questions that we have to ask you, if you don't mind."

I'm so tired.

"Now I understand if you want a lawyer present. We can arrange for one if you'd like."

I don't answer.

"Aaron, this will go a lot easier for all of us if you just talk with us," Griffin states.

Again, I'm silent.

Fisher leans forwards. "Look, kid. I get you're worried about your friend. You're not in trouble. At least not at the moment. We just need to figure out exactly what happened back in that apartment, ok?"

I got Zoë hurt. That's what happened.

"Aaron?" Griffin tried to get my attention.

"Ask your questions," I croak.

They look at each other and shake their heads. Griffin looks back at me.

"What were you doing in that apartment?" he asks.

"I was there to get my friend and take her home."

"Your friend being Zoë St. John?" Fisher asks.

I nod my head.

"And why were you trying to take her home?" Griffin asks.

"Because her dad was worried about her. He hadn't heard from her in a week. If you check, you'll find that he filed a missing person's report for her yesterday," I answer.

"We know that. Just asking the questions," Griffin says. "What was the issue that led to the incident?"

"I don't understand."

"What made you and Deacon fight?" Fisher clarifies.

"He was mad that I'd convinced Zoë to leave. He didn't like me and didn't want Zoë to leave him." I take a drink of water. "He was already upset after we'd fought earlier that day. He'd attacked me," I hold up my hands, "just to be clear. So, when Zoë was leaving, he'd grabbed her. I pushed him and he drew a gun. After that, it was all a blur. Next thing you know, I'm on my back staring up at the ceiling lights. Deacon had gotten pulled off of me and when I immediately looked for Zoë. Once I saw in that she'd been shot, I tried to stop the bleeding, while that guy call you."

"That guy being Marshal Alenko?" Griffin says.

"Yes." I confirm.

"I see, so you were just defending yourself?"

"Yes," voice cracks, "I didn't mean for any of this to happen. Things just got out of hand."

"It's ok, Aaron. We understand." Griffin soothes. "Unfortunately, this sort of thing happens all the time in this city."

"Am I gonna go to jail?" My voice wavers. "I didn't mean for any of this to happen. I was just trying to help my friend. I don't want to go to jail."

"Easy, son. You're fine." Griffin sooths. "You're not going to jail. Right now, we are just trying to figure out what happened."

"For now, you are going to be detained here," Fisher speaks up. "However, that is just until we have testimonies from the other witnesses. Mr. Winters has his story to tell, as does Mr. Alenko and Miss. St. John. After that, we'll be able to know who to charge and what to charge them for."

I wipe away tears that have started to flood my vision. "Ok."

"But for now, as we said, we'll have to hold you. At least for forty-eight hours Fisher continues. "In the meantime, you still have your one phone call."

The detectives stand up and a police officer enters the room. The officer uncuffs me from the table and leads me to the payphone, where I call my mom. She answers the phone and is, of course, worried about me. Mr. St. John had gotten a phone call from the hospital and was told what had happened. My mom asked if I was ok and I lied, saying that I was. I explained what had happened briefly. She tells me everything will be ok and that she will get the money together for bail.

After that, I hang up the phone. The officer leads me down the cellblock and gives me my own cozy cell. The walls are made of dark gray bricks and the cell is barren except for a tiny cot and chrome toilet. Seeing no other choice, I lay down on the cot and within seconds the dreaded fog of sleep overtakes me.

Chapter 15

A plastic cup of soda is placed down on a tray that lays on my lap. I look up to see a stewardess staring blankly down at me. She turns and starts to walk away, down the aisle towards the back of the plane. I look to my left and find myself alone in my row of seats. The window is closed. I sit up and look around. The plane is completely empty. I look back to the window and decide to open it.

The shudder snaps open the instant I touch it. Light floods my eyes and I hold up my hand to shield my eyes. As they adjust, I hear glass shatter. I jump from my seat and scan the cabin once more. The plane remains empty and the previous silence returns. I sit back down in my seat and look back at the window but am shocked to find it is closed again. I'm about to reach over and open it again when I'm interrupted by the stewardess.

Without a word said or sound made, she places a plastic cup of soda down on the tray that lays across my lap. I stare at her, confused and am only given a blank look in response. She turns and starts to walk away, down the aisle towards the back of the plane. I watch her walk away until she disappears behind a curtain.

What the?

I look back to the window and am surprised to find that instead of two empty seats between me and the window, there are now two big men. They look as though they walked right out of the *Matrix*. With the exception that they seem to be body builders in their spare time. I look past the men at the window then back at them. In the second that I look away from them, they violently warp in their seats; their heads turned to stare directly at me.

"Can we help you?" they ask me, their voices full of malice.

I shake my head at them, and they slowly turn their heads to face forwards. I go to stand up again when I'm stopped by the stewardess once more. Calmly, she lays a plastic cup of soda onto the tray that stretches across my lap. I notice that the first couple of cups she'd given me have disappeared. I look up at her and am greeted by her lifeless gaze. She turns and walks back down the aisle, disappearing behind a curtain.

I look to my right to find the on the opposite row of seats there now sits an old woman who has a cloud of makeup surrounding her as she dabs a sponge on her face. Beside her sit two little kids: a boy, and a girl. The boy looks about eight or nine, with short red hair and is covered in freckles. While the girl looks a bit older, maybe twelve. Her hair is long and blond, twisted into twin ponytails. They both stare at me with glassy, black eyes.

"Can we help you?" they ask. I shake my head and they look forwards, their movement slow, almost robotic.

Ok, fuck this.

I try to get up out of my chair, only to find now I'm buckled in. I reach down to unbuckle myself when the stewardess reappears. She holds a plastic cup of soda in her hands and stares down at me with her soulless eyes.

"Is there a problem, sir?" she asks.

"Ok, I'm done." I unbuckle the seatbelt and stand up, flipping my now cleared tray up. "Look whatever the Dullahan had planned here, I'm over it."

The stewardess tilts her head. "I'm not sure I understand."

"Oh, come on, what was he trying to do? Bore me to death?" I shout at her. "The time loop, the strange men in suits and the creep little kids. This is the best he's got?"

"Sir, please. I'm sorry if you are not satisfied with your service. If you would like I can bring over the captain to hear your complaint." The stewardess's voice is like the others, full of hatred.

"Whatever, out of my way." I push the stewardess to the side. The soda in her hand spills over her.

I start to walk towards the front of the plane. As I do, I see the cabin is now full of people, all of them staring at me. In one of the seats is a shadow man. A pang of familiarity forces me to slow as I walk past him. I stare intently at him, hoping to understand who he is. Before I can see anything, the windows of the plane all snap shut all around me, making the cabin dark. As my eyes adjust, I see that the shadow man has disappeared. I try to ignore the people as I continue walking, the cabin silent as though everyone is holding their breath. I reach the door to the plane and read the instructions for how to open it in case of emergencies. At least, I try.

The words on the side of the door are written in hieroglyphs. Numbers, letters, and symbols form together in sentences, and I cannot make out a single word. Frustrated, I reach down and pull what looks to be the handle upwards. The door to the cabin is then violently ripped away from the rest of the plane and light pours in, blinding me.

I shut my eyes, but the light is too strong. Forcing its way through my eyelids. I place my hands over my eyes and rub them fiercely. The light starts to dim and the pain in my eyes fades along with it. I open my eyes again only to be dismayed as I watch the stewardess place a fresh cup of soda on the tray that stretches out before me.

Enraged, I slap the cup away, sending it flying over the stewardess and the old woman in the opposite row. The old woman pays me no attention while the stewardess looks down at me. I glare up at her and my heart skips a beat. Having gotten used to seeing her soulless expression, seeing her eyebrows furled and jaw clenched startles me.

"Is there a problem with your drink? Sir." The word sir coming out with a sinister hiss.

I take a second to compose myself. "I want off this fucking plane."

"We're sorry." The entire cabin speaks in unison. "We can't let you do that."

I press down on the release of my seatbelt. Before the buckle even leaves my hand, the click rings out through the cabin of the plane and instantly the people start to attack me. The two matrix extras grab me and hold me down while the little kids clamber over the old lady, who still hasn't stopped doing her makeup. The little kids along with the stewardess start to attack me. Punch, clawing, and biting me. Other people on the plane fight over each other as they try to get at me. I feel someone behind me grab my hair. An Asian woman wearing a black leather jacket jumps over the crowd of people and stabs me in the chest with what looks to be a nail file.

I try to struggle, but even if the *Matrix* body builders weren't holding me down, I am being buried under a sea of people. As people attack me, I try to imagine a way out of here. I struggle to focus through the pain and panic. Without much choice, I force myself to go limp. The kids start to claw at my face, and I squint my eyes in a desperate attempt to protect them.

I feel my muscles relax as I try to imagine a way out of here. I picture the plane from *World War Z* and how

Brad Pitt detonated a grenade on board, creating a massive hole that sucked everything out of the plane.

Everything that wasn't buckled anyways.

Still clutching my seatbelt, I strain my arms against the horde of people on top of me. Over the shouting and clamoring of the people trying to kill me, I hear a snap as my seatbelt locks into place. As the snap rings out through the air, a massive hole is ripped away from the plane where the two children were sitting.

The cabin instantly depressurizes and everything that isn't strapped down out gets sucked out. Within seconds, I'm alone in the plane. I look over at the massive hole in the plane and am horrified to find that in the place of the old lady that ignored me throughout, now sits the Dullahan. He holds his spine whip tightly in his hand, his head resting in his lap, unaffected by the intense wind flying through the cabin. His head faces me and his eyes glow faintly behind his squinted eyelids.

"Not bad, Aaron," he says calmly. "Not bad at all. I'm starting to be impressed."

Not looking to give him the satisfaction, I picture the plane splitting in half, right down the middle. With a loud groan and a cracking of steel, the plane splits in half, sending me and the Dullahan spiraling away from each other.

As my half of the plane falls from the sky, I picture a parachute on my back. The chair I'm strapped to starts to warp and shift around me. Shrinking and compressing into a large parachute bag. The second it finishes I'm lifted off into the air and watch in awe as my half of the plane sinks to the ground below me. I reach up and pull the cord on my parachute. With a satisfying rip, the back opens and my freefall suddenly becomes gentler.

As I slide through the air, the ground racing up towards me. I look around, expecting to see the Dullahan riding a dragon or some shit like that. I'm relieved when no such thing appears. However, all around me is nothing but pure white light. My eyes once more start to burn and I squint through them, refusing to let the Dullahan catch me while blind.

As I descend from the sky, I form a pair of sunglasses around my eyes. Not a moment after they appear, they ripped away by an intense wind. I sigh with frustration and start to form goggles instead. Finally able to see without fear of going blind, I look down below.

The ground rapidly rises towards me. In every direction I feel as though I am looking at a new world. I see a vast, endless ocean far off to my left. Just before it I see a desert with hills and mountains forming and tumbling over only to build themselves back up again. To my right I see a dense forest wrapping around a massive city. The city was easily twice the size of Chicago, maybe larger.

I look behind me to see a sea of blood thrashing around. The waves of blood smacking against a black beach. I look in front of me and see a mountain rising out of the ground. Its peak scrapping against the sky. Directly below me is a swamp. The air above it already beginning to make me gag as its rotten stench reaches my nose.

I slowly fall through the air towards the swamp. I try to direct myself towards the ocean, towards Finnan. But the wind fights me, keeping me above the swamp. Sensing the pointlessness of fighting, I wait for the swamp to swallow me once more.

***

I'm about 500 feet in the air when I hear the snapping of a whip. I twist around, looking for the source. The snap rings out again and I look up above me. Racing downwards towards me in his horse drawn carriage is the Dullahan, his head held high in the air.

"Aaron Ward!" he shouts, his voice akin to thunder.

The wind starts to fly in every direction all around me. I look around, hoping to find something. Anything to help me against him. Then it hits me.

I have anything I could ever need!

In my hands, I picture a large shield. The Dullahan lets fly his whip towards me just as my shield appears. The whip collides with it and a flash of lightning rips through the air. The smell of ozone fills my nose as I'm sent spinning away from the impact, helpless. I see no other choice as the Dullahan rears back his arm, preparing to let fly his whip once more. I picture a long dagger in my hand and with one swipe over my head, I cut the strings of my parachute.

I plummet towards the swamp below. The trees seem to grow taller, racing up to meet me as I fall past them. As I do so, the Dullahan's whip cracks at the air behind me. I see the water of the swamp rapidly approaching and I brace for impact.

I hit the water at some unknown speed. All over, I feel bones break as my skin burns with fury. I sink into the muddy, rotten water. Shock takes me as I start to choke, the water having flooded down my throat as I cried out in pain. Deeper into the water I sink, unable to move. Unable to think about anything but trying to breathe.

All over, my body screams in protest as I try to swim upwards towards the surface. My legs don't respond, and my arms are too heavy to do more than flail hopelessly. I stare up at the water's surface, the light from the

Dullahan's eyes rips through the murky water. Like lightning trapped in a bottle.

 I think about my mom. About Chloe and Jake. *I think about how I'll never get to see them again. How I'll never be able to explain what happened to me. What I did to Deacon. Why I did it. I'll never see Chloe's warm smile again. Or hear Jake's laugh. I'll never hug my mom again, never getting to hear her complain about her day at work or her dreams of my future.*

 Most of all, I'll never get to see Zoë again. I'll never get to tell her how sorry I was. For pushing her away after she rejected me. I'll never get to tell her how I truly feel about her. I won't see her steel gray eyes light up at the sight of mischief to be had. Never get to hear her complain about her brother or dad. Never hear her voice again.

 Despair washes over me. I'll never get to live a life worth living. Never go to college. Never move in with the girl I love. I'll never know what my kids would've looked like. Never hear their laughs. I'll never have truly lived my life. Never done more than just exist day to day.

***

I'm sitting around a large table outside. The air is warm and soft, the shade of a large willow tree shields me from the rays of the sun. The sky is almost clear, with a single large cloud floating off in the distance. I look around me and see my friends and family eating what looks to be Thanksgiving dinner. Time moves in slow motion as I stare at them.

 I see my mom; she has Jake bouncing on her knee and he laughs away as my late cousin Brian gives him a goofy face from across the table. Besides him sits my sister, who laughs at a joke Zoë's just told her. Zoë's mouth is half full of mashed potatoes. I reach out my arm to touch her, realizing immediately that my body is healed. No broken bones or anything. I smile, relieved and continue to look around. I see my aunt Katrina and my great aunt Claudia. The two smile warmly at me before talking to each other.

Finnan is here, too. He has his arm wrapped around a beautiful woman. Her hair is jet black and her eyes, as green as grass. She smiles, laying her head on his shoulders as he speaks to other member of my friends and family. I see some of my other friends from school, along with cousins and distant relatives I've met from the many funerals I'd attended. All around me, the table seems to stretch onwards forever, seating all those I'd considered family. Across from me, sits my dad. He smiles at me, his eyes warm and inviting.

"Hello, Aaron."

"Dad?" I ask. "Where are we?"

"I'm not entirely sure." He looks to my mom, his eyes lighting up with joy. "But I consider it paradise."

"Paradise?" I echo. "Am I dead?"

"I'm not sure. Are you?" He looks away from my mom to my sister.

"Last thing I saw…"

My dad doesn't listen, instead he looks at Zoë, a coy grin spreads across his face. "Boy son, you sure know how to pick 'em."

I look at Zoë. For a moment I'm distracted by her. Time seems to have frozen completely now. She's pointing her spoon of mash potatoes at Jake, her mouth open in laughter. I look at Jake to see he's spilt gravy all over himself. I look back at Zoë, guilt burning in my chest as I remember her getting hurt. I look back to my dad.

"But if you're here with me, then wouldn't I be dead?" I ask him.

"I don't know," he says, taking a bite of turkey. "I don't know enough about how this all works."

"Well, what do you know then?" I raise my voice in frustration.

"I know that I'm here, on this perfect day. With my family and friends all around me eating good food. No one's arguing. No one's hurt. Nothing is hurting me." He looks back at my mom. "I'm at peace."

"But what about me?" I ask him. "I can't be dead."

"Why's that?" my dad asks, not looking away from my mom.

"Because I can't be!" I start to panic. "I have to live. I have so much I haven't gotten to do. People I need to see." I look to Jake. "If I'm dead then Jake's next in line! I can't let him die dad!" My dad looks away from my mom, a confused look on his face.

"I see," he says. "You're right." He looks around at the sky. As though he's seeing it for the first time. "You shouldn't be here, son."

"I know, Dad, that's what I've been saying." I lean forwards.

"No, Aaron. You don't understand." He looks at me, fear in his eyes. "You shouldn't be here! He's coming!"

"The Dullahan?" I ask. "Where?"

At the mention of the Dullahan the temperature drops around us. The wind picks up and the willow tree behind my dad starts to shake.

"No. Not him," My dad states urgently.

"Then who dad? Who is coming?" I start to shout as the wind grows stronger and louder.

Around us, I notice my friends and family have been starring at us. Their faces frozen in a mixture of fear and hatred. Brian's eyes go wide with terror, blood beginning to flow from them. The gravy on Jake turns into blood. My mom stares at my dad with malice.

"You have to go, now!" My dad stands up from the table. When he does, Zoë lunches at him from across the table. She screams and grunts like a zombie.

"Dad!" I jump out of my seat. "Where do I go? What do I do?"

The wind stings my skin as it spins and tears around me. The food and tableware start to be knocked over and carried away by the wind. My friends and family start to stand up, their faces either one of horror or rage. Jake jumps on Brian, stabbing him savagely with a fork.

"Aaron!" My dad's voice rips through the air. "You need to wake up!"

The wind starts to push against me, lifting my up into the air. I grab onto the table, digging my fingers into the wood. My dad is now surrounded by everyone at the table.

"DAD!" I scream at him.

"Aaron!" Brian's voice calls out. "You need to go!" The members of my family and friends begin to pile on top of them both. "Whatever you do-"

I don't get to hear the rest as the wind howls in my ears. I feel my fingers slipping and within seconds I start to fly through the air. I reach out at grab onto a branch from the willow. I hold on for dear life as I look down at my dad and Brian. I scream out for them.

"Aaron!" Their voices whisper in my ear in unison. "Don't trust Finnan."

And with that, I'm sent flying away through the air.

Chapter 16

"Ward!"

I jolt awake, so violently in fact that I fall out of bed. I hit the ground hard, my head bouncing off the stone floor. Groaning, I look up at the police officer that stands at the cell door.

"Jesus, kid." He winces at me. "That must've hurt."

I groan weakly in response.

"Come on, get up."

"Where are we going?" I ask.

"You've got a visitor."

***

I enter the visitor's room and am immediately pulled into a hug by my mom. I hug her back for as long as I can until she pushes my away, holding onto my face.

"Oh, Aaron. Are you ok?" she gushes. "You had me so worried!"

"I'm fine, mom. Just tired," I assure her.

I look to the table in the room and see a stout man with a thin mustache and balding head staring at me through half-moon glasses. He stands up and offers me his hand.

"James Moore." I take his hand and he shakes firmly, "I'm your attorney."

I look at my mom. "You hired a lawyer?"

"Of course, I did!" she replies.

"Can we afford a lawyer?" I ask.

"Actually," James interjects, "I'm doing this case gratis."

"Really?" I ask.

"Your aunt Katrina is an old friend from college," he informs me. "She called in a favor, and I couldn't say no."

"Ok, well. Great."

"Please, let sit." He sits back down at the table, which has folders and papers sprawled across it. "We have much to discuss."

***

James and I speak about the situation I'm in. My mom sits quietly at the table; I could tell none of this was easy for her.

Her son was fighting death every time he closed his eyes and now, he was in jail for killing a guy. What kind of mother would she be if she wasn't worried?

According to James, the case seemed to be going my way. So far, the police had uncovered that Deacon had cocaine in his apartment as well as the gun was unregistered. Then there were the testimonies, which also seemed to be going my way. My story was believable and understandable, just a concerned friend looking for his missing friend. Then there was the neighbor, Marshal, and his story. How he told it, he seemed to believe everything I told him, and when he had arrived, he had already heard several gunshots before pulling Deacon, a twenty something guy from a bruised and bloody teenager.

As well as with none of my fingerprints on the gun, it was clear that Deacon was the one who shot Zoë. Unfortunately, as this all happened in Deacon's house, it could be suggested that I went there with malicious intent and had instigated the fight. That was the story Deacon told, that he used his gun in self defense and that it was my fault Zoë got shot.

Which it was.

"But what about Zoë?" I ask James. "I mean, she was there, she knows what really happened."

"Yes, that is what you and I are banking on." James pushes his glasses into place. "As of right now, it is Zoë's testimony that will decide if you are going to be charged with breaking and entering as well as assault or if Deacon will be charged with assault. Regardless, he is already in trouble thanks to his gun and drugs."

"What if her testimony isn't enough?" my mom asks.

"From where I'm standing, I feel that if Aaron is telling the truth and Zoë does as well, that's unlikely." James smiles reassuringly. "However, if such a situation does come to pass, I believe there is a 100 percent guarantee that a jury would take your side in court."

"I was there to help Zoë, not hurt Deacon." I reiterate. "Zoë's testimony will confirm that."

"I hope so, son."

"So, if he does go to jail," my mom asks, "how long will his sentence be?"

"In the unbelievable case where Aaron is charged, the maximum sentencing in ten years in jail." James leans back in his chair and rubs his eyes. "But again, I believe with absolute certainty that Aaron will not be charged. Officially, regardless of intention towards Deacon Winters,

Aaron was there looking for his friend who was reported missing by her father. He was the one who was assaulted initially, and he was also shot by Deacon. Add all that with cooperating with the police and I say again that he will walk free." James reaches for a glass of water on the table and takes a long drink before continuing.

"So, when will we know?" I ask.

"When Miss. St. John is well enough the police will speak with her and get her statement on what happened," James answers. "I do believe they will be speaking with her sometime later today."

"She's awake already?" I practically leap out of my chair.

"Yes, she is, honey. Her dad said she made it out of surgery without any problems," My mom tells me.

"I mean, is she going to be ok?"

"They're expecting a full recovery," she says.

I fall back into my seat, relief washing over me.

She's going to be ok!

I look back to James. "So, when do you think I'll be let go?"

He smiles. "Given that no charges have been officially labeled against you, they will have to release you tomorrow."

"That soon?" my mom asks.

"Yep, the law states that the police can only hold you without charges for a maximum of twenty-four hours."

"Oh, that's good." My mom sighs with relief.

"I guess that's it then," I conclude.

"Right." James stands up and starts packing up his papers that he has strewn across the table. "I must say, I'm happy Katrina reached out to me."

"You are?" I ask.

"Of course, I'm always happy to help a friend. Or in this case, family of a friend." James shoves his belongings into a briefcase. "Once I heard about what had happened, I knew I could get you off. Any other lawyer you could've gone to would've charged you an arm and a leg. But this," he waves his hand is dismissal through the air, "was nothing."

"Well, I'm truly grateful for all you help." I stand up and shake his hand. "I really thought I was screwed."

"Just be careful, we're not out of the woods yet." James warns. "But yes, I do think this is an open and shut case. And of course, it was my pleasure."

A guard walks into the room.

"I guess it's time for me to leave," my mom says to me.

"I know," I reply.

My mom pulls me into a tight hug. She leans in and whispers in my ear.

"I'm so proud of you."

I tighten my hug a bit in response. After that, my mom and James are led out of the building. At the same time, I am led back to my cell, where I spend the rest of my day.

***

The guards provided me with a book to read to help pass time. In between eating and some time out of my cell in the common area, I read *Dante's Inferno*. Honestly, the book was better than I'd expected. But the longer I read it, the more I felt like Dante as he sank deeper into Hell. From where I stood now, I felt as though I was preparing to come out the other side. Ready to enter Heaven and cast off my old life. The guards had also provided me with a change of clothes. Sure, they were prisoners' clothes, but they were better than the bloody mess than I was wearing when they brought me in.

The day grew late and before I knew it night had arrived. Sleep clawed at my eyes to the point that I could not read any further. Determined not to fall asleep until I was out of jail, I found myself working out. My scarred and raw body screamed in protest for every second as the night dragged on. At one point, a guard came by and demanded to know why I wasn't asleep.

"I can't sleep, sir," I respond. "Too anxious."

"Is that right?" he asks in a condescending tone. "Well, I don't care if you can't sleep. But every second you spend out of bed is another second of yard time you lose tomorrow. Now, GET IN YOUR BED!"

With a defeated sigh, I climb into bed. As I push myself off the floor, the guard takes notice of my scars.

"Jesus, boy! What happened to you?"

"Just a rough life, sir."

Just play it cool. You'll be out of here tomorrow.

I didn't blame the guard for being mean to me. As far as he knew, I was just another scumbag who'd broken the law and hurt innocent people. He was just doing his job. Regardless of whether or not I was innocent, what would be the point of fighting him? After I laid in bed, the guard watched me for a minute. Eventually, he walked on, checking the other cells.

The night dragged on after that. I remembered the hospital and the week I sent fighting sleep. It was easier there. There were noises I could focus on. People I could talk too. T.V. to watch. But here, there was nothing. If there was anything good about prison I would say, it would be that a good night's sleep was easily found.

***

The ground I lay on is soggy and sticky. The air; putrid and thick. My nose is running as the humidity sends my sinuses into overdrive. I stare up through the many trees of the swamp to see the night sky. The stars smile down at me as a chill runs down my spine.

"You sure are resilient, aren't you?" The Dullahan's voice brings a fierce wind.

I sit up and look to my left, where the Dullahan stands. He has his whip strapped at his waist, his head in one hand and a brush in another. Beside him are his carriage and the horses that pull it. He brushes his horses softly, flakes of dead, rotten flesh peeling away with clumps of hair.

"How am I alive?" I ask.

"You aren't." He finishes brushing his horse and turns his body, his head held up to face me. "At least, not completely."

"Enough with being cryptic. Just be straight with me," I growl at him. "I'm tired of guessing."

"Fair enough." The Dullahan purses his lips, his brown furled in thought. "Twice now you should be dead."

"Twice?"

"You should've died every time you've slept but each time you've managed to run away or be saved." The Dullahan's head scowls, "By either that amulet of yours or..."

"By Finnan."

"Yes. Finnan." The Dullahan spits. "Twice now I've had you. The first time when you looked at my eyes." His eyes twitch and I shut mine instantly. He chuckles and I open them again, looking away from him now.

"And the second time?" I ask.

"When you drowned here."

I stare at water of the swamp and feel another chill run through me. "So how am I still alive?"

"Finnan." The Dullahan walks forwards and sits beside me. He places his head in his lap, facing it upwards towards me. Every fiber of my being screams at me to run. But I don't.

I need to hear what he has to say.

"What deal did you make with him?" I ask, careful not to look at his eyes.

"It is not for me to tell you." The Dullahan sighs. "I do wish I could, but only he can. It's just how it is."

"But he did make a deal with you, one that allows you to hunt and kill my family. Right?"

"Correct," he answers.

"But I thought you made a deal with someone else?" I accuse him. "That whenever someone of my family-"

"-ever sat on the throne of Ireland." The Dullahan cuts me off. "A useful lie Finnan conjured up to ensure the members of his line never uncovered the truth."

"Why?" I demand. "What does he get out of it? What do you get for killing my family? How does this pact benefit you?"

The Dullahan is silent for a moment as he chooses his words. All around me, the swamp seems to grow louder as the wind dies down. The air grows more fowl and I feel as though something is watching me.

Not something. Many different things.

"I am a demon," the Dullahan declares. "But I'm not immortal. Though I cannot be killed by the likes of you humans, I can die. To ensure this doesn't happen, I must feed. But I do not feed on the flesh of God's creatures. Nor the plants that cover the earth."

"Human souls." I whisper, the uneasy feeling of the swamp growing.

"Indeed." The Dullahan calmly grabs the spine whip from his waist. "Now I can take the souls of any I wish. With how many people there now are in the world, I could feast like never before. But it wasn't so easy thousands of years ago."

"So, you made a deal."

"Yes, I made a deal." The Dullahan agrees. "One that would give a single man everything he could ever want, while ensuring I could feast on his family line forever."

"But why my family? How does this benefit you if you still have to hunt us in our dreams?"

"Therein lies my curse." The Dullahan grips the whip tightly. "It was supposed to be a simple culling. I would devour the men of you family one by one as they slept. However, I was tricked. Finnan had arranged the pact in such a way that I would still have to hunt those I sought. As well as I could not hunt any other until his line was wiped out." The Dullahan stands up, all around me noises of shuffling feet and heavy breathing ring out. "And he has done well in ensuring I could not finish his line. Something that should've taken a decade at most ended up taking centuries."

"Can't it be stopped?" I ask, standing up myself. "I mean, what if I was able to make Finnan end the pact, wouldn't that set you free?"

"He never would. Even after his death, he still enjoys the gifts I gave him centuries ago. He would never end it." The wind begins to pick up once more, chilling me to the bone.

"Let me try!" I shout over the wind. "What's the harm in letting me try? Don't I deserve a chance at least?" The Dullahan doesn't reply. I take care not to look him in the eyes as I turn and face him, "Why are you telling me all this? All this time you've spent speaking to me, you could've been trying harder to kill me. Why?"

The Dullahan sighs, "Because I'm tired of killing your family. In my time I've gotten to know each and every one of your line and I've grown to respect my prey. It is for this reason I have chosen to speak to you. Because you deserve to know why it is you are about to die."

The wind tumbles around me. In the shadows of the swamp, I sense the tension in the Dullahan's forces as they prepare to attack.

I need to wake up.

The Dullahan slowly raises his head into the air. At the same time, he lifts the whip into the air behind his shoulder, preparing to strike.

Wake up!

The wind howls in my ears. All around me, the rumbling of footsteps as creatures charge me from the shadows of the swamp. The Dullahan's whip snaps forwards at me, his eyes opening and flooding the swamp with white-hot light.

WAKE UP!

***

"WAKE UP!" The guard screams at me.

I sit up in my bed with a scream of terror. My body is caked in sweat, my breathing ragged and shallow. I look forwards at the guard and seem him standing in the doorway of my now open cell. Light shines in from a window in the walkway behind him.

"Finally!" the guard shouts. "I thought I was going to have to drag you out of that bed."

"Sorry." I pant. "Deep sleeper."

The guard looks at me with curiosity. "Bad dream?"

I smile. "I've had worse."

"Ok." The guard shakes his head. "Come on, let's go."

"Where to?" I ask, hopping out of bed.

"You're begin released," the guard answers.

"Wait, really?" I say through on my shirt.

"Yes, really." The guard turns to me. "Are you coming or what?"

***

Zoë's statement cleared me. The police compared it to mine and, with the evidence against Deacon, I was officially cleared of any charges. The police escorted me out of the jailhouse through the main station and handed me off to my mom, who had thankfully brought me a change of clothes. With her was my sister and Jake. Chloe could barely look at me and I knew why.

She's still mad that I won't tell her what's going on with me.

Mr. St. John was there as well. He took my hand and pulled me into a hug.

"Thank you." He speaks softly in my ear. "Thank you for getting my daughter." He pulls away from me.

"I'm sorry about what happened."

"No, don't you dare be sorry." He stops me. "This is not your fault. Its mine. For not keeping a closer eye on her. For letting her hang out with that sonofabitch, Deacon." He trails off. His eyes are full of regret.

"You're a good dad," I tell him. "She didn't do any of this because you weren't. She just, doesn't know what she wants from her life. But Deacon, he gave her something exciting. Something that she never got with me or from you."

"So, you think she did this to herself?" His tone is a mixture of guilt and anger.

"I think," I pick my words carefully, "that to blame anyone but Deacon for what happened isn't going to make anything better."

"He's right, Willard." My mom steps in. "I think you should head back to the hospital. She should be with her father right now."

He nods his head, then looks at me. "You can come with, if you'd like."

I shake my head. "I'm not so sure that's a good idea."

"Nonsense," he scoffs. "You're the only thing she's talked about since she woke up."

I look at my mom, and she nods her head in understanding. I hug her and shake the hair on Jake's head. He laughs at me. I look at Chloe and feel daggers as she glares at me. I look back to Mr. St. John:

"Can you give me a few minutes? I need to talk to my sister in private."

He nods his head and Chloe hands Jake over to my mom. We both walk towards my mom's car. When we get there, she crosses her arms and cocks her head.

"You finally gonna tell me what's happening with you?"

"Yes." I reply. "But before I do, I need you to promise never to tell anyone. And you need to listen to the whole story before you can ask me any questions."

"Just tell me!" She snaps.

I tell her everything. About the nightmares. About Dullahan and the curse. I tell her about Finnan. I explain why I went away to see Aunt Claudia. My scars. Everything. When I'm finished. the look on her face tells me all I need to know.

She thinks I'm crazy.

"So that's what happened to Brian?" she asks. "To Dad?"

"To every male member of our family." I clarify.

"And when you die…" she can't finish her sentence.

"Jake is next," I finish for her.

"Aaron, this is crazy!" She starts to laugh in disbelief, "I mean, you can't be serious thinking I believe any of this."

"Chloe, in what world would I just make this up?" I ask her. "What could I be doing that is so bad that I would just pull all of this out of my ass?"

"I don't know, drugs or something?" she rationalizes.

"Chloe, I'm not lying. If I was, would I be covered in the same type of scars as Brian was. As Dad?"

Chloe goes silent for a minute, trying to find a way to call me crazy still. But finally, she caves, "So, what can you do?"

"The only thing I can do. Try and make Finnan end the pact. If I can do that, then the Dullahan doesn't have to kill me or Jake. This will all end."

"And if he doesn't?"

"I'll make sure he will," I promise her.

Chloe is quiet for a minute as she processes everything. I prepare for her to call me insane. Threaten to send me away like Aunt Claudia. But instead, she just hugs me. I hug her back and we stand there for a moment. I didn't realize how much I need a hug. My body relaxed and I felt tears start to pool in my eyes, Chloe pushes herself away and looks into my eyes.

"You do whatever it is that you have to. Just promise me that nothing will happen to Jake."

I nod me head. "I promise."

Tears have started to run down her cheeks. She wipes them away and starts off towards mom. I turn and follow her. Reunited with mom and Mr. St. John, I hug my mom goodbye and leave with Mr. St. John for the hospital.

I'm coming Zoë.

Chapter 17

I follow Mr. St. John down a long hallway. The hospital is overflowing with people. From what I overhear, there was a horrible accident recently. Apparently, a semi-truck's brakes failed. A lot of people I passed were either in shock with minor injuries or looked the way I constantly felt.

At death's door.

Finally, Mr. St. John comes to a stop outside of one of the rooms. He turns to look at me and with a smile, opens the door. I follow him inside and see Zoë in her bed. If it wasn't for her messy hair and the hospital gown, I'd say she looked as good as ever before.

At first, I think she's asleep. Her head rests on her shoulder and her eyes are closed. But as her dad closes the door behind me, she lifts her head and looks to me. Her steel gray eyes stare right through me. I'm about to say something, but the words won't come out. Her dad takes a seat beside her bed.

"Hey there, sweetie," her dad says softly. "How are you doing?"

"Fine," she croaks in response, her eyes not leaving me. "Aaron?"

"Hey." I smile weakly. "You're looking good."

She chuckles at that. "I feel like I just got shot."

I chuckle along with her. Her dad smiles. She turns to look at him.

"Can you give us a bit?" she asks him.

He nods his head and stands up. As he passes me, he gives me a warm look. He steps out of the room, closing the door behind him. I go ahead and take his seat by Zoë's bed. The room is quiet for a bit. Neither of us knows where to start.

"What happened with Deacon?" Zoë asks finally.

"What do you mean?" I ask.

"He's in trouble, right?"

My words catch in my throat. I cough and explain what happened. Why I was there, what happened before I'd gotten there. My fight with Deacon and him locking me in his basement. I tell her how Deacon beat me, and how I miraculously didn't get knocked out. I mention Marshal and how he saved me, then I tell her about my couple nights in jail. How I never stopped thinking about her.

"So, you're not in trouble anymore?" she asks.

"Not anymore, thanks to you. Thanks to your statement, the police felt I was acting in self-defense. Deacon attacked me. He shot you. They didn't feel the need to keep me any longer."

"So, it's all over then," she says with a distant tone.

"Look, I'm sorry." My hands start to shake. "I'm sorry that I got mad at you, outside the hospital. I'm sorry about Deacon; I know you liked him."

"Aaron," she starts to say.

"No just, please," I beg her. "You liked him, and I got in your way of that. But I'm also not sorry that I did. He isn't a good guy, Zoë. If you'd heard and seen the things I had about him, you would understand."

"Aaron," she stops me. "Stop saying you're sorry. It's not your fault. None of this is."

She tries to sit up straighter and grimaces in pain. Guilt once more tugs at my stomach. Once she settles back down, she continues.

"I pushed you away. Back at the hospital because I thought you were just jealous of Deacon. I was mad at my dad for always choosing my brother over me. And I had no one else to go to but Deacon. I was reckless. The entire time I was at his apartment he was just so sweet and supportive of me. We drank and smoked a lot." She starts to tear up a bit. "But the entire time I was with him I felt like something was off. I kept thinking about what you had said about him. And the more I did, the more I realized you were right."

"So, why didn't you leave?" I ask.

"Because I furious." She wipes away a tear that started to fall down her cheek. "Not at you or my dad. But myself. All you did was care for me. Support me. And I pushed you away for some asshole. And I don't even know why I did it."

"You can't be that hard on yourself." I tell her. "We're still kids, we both will make plenty of mistakes. You thought you found a good guy; how could you have known otherwise?"

"Because you kept telling me." She wipes more tears away. "I should've believed you. Should've listened to you. I'm sorry."

"Stop." I beg her. "Stop blaming yourself. It doesn't help anyone, not now."

Zoë sniffles, wiping away more tears. With her free hand, she takes mine and holds in tightly. I grip her hand in response. The two of us are silent for a moment. Taking the time to compose ourselves.

"At least my dad won't have to worry about throwing me a birthday party." Zoë smiles.

Birthday party?

Zoë looks at me and laughs dryly.

"Don't tell me you forgot?"

Oh, shit!

"Um." I try to come up with something to say.

"It's ok." Zoë eases. "I forgot, too, for a while. Only remembered this morning when my brother mentioned it."

"I'm sorry, I knew it was tomorrow, I just-"

"Like it said, it's ok." Zoë laughs. "I'm not mad at all."

"Well, now I've got to think of a gift to get you." I smile. "I mean, after all, it has to be good enough for your eighteenth."

"Eighteen years old." Zoë stars off in the distance for a moment, lost in thought. "I can't believe it."

The smiles on our faces grow wider. Hers with joy, mine because of her. Then, a pang of dread sings out in my chest. And I'm reminded of what's been happening to me.

"Zoë, there's something I need to tell you."

"Is it about all these scars you have?" she asks, rubbing her thumb across my bandaged knuckles.

"Kind of, yeah."

I take a deep breath and tell her everything. About the nightmares and the Dullahan. The curse and Finnan. I leave no detail out. When I finish, I find myself out of breath. Zoë's eyes are now dry and puffy from crying. Her hand still gripping mine tightly.

"Aaron." She seems lost for words. "I don't know what to say to all that."

"I'm not making any of it up, I swear to God."

"I don't think you are but," she shakes her head, "It's all so much to take in."

"Yeah." I hang my head. "Trust me, I know."

"So, is there a way you can stop it?"

"Maybe." I look back at her. I swear every time I see her eyes, I fall in love with her all over again. "But it's a long shot. I might not live much longer."

Zoë slaps my hand, though the bandages my knuckles sting as though I'd just punched a wall.

"Ouch!" I yelp.

"You better not die on me Aaron!" she commands. "I'm not sure if this shit you're telling me is real or in your head. But whatever it is you better damn well deal with it."

I smile warmly. *She certainly has a way with words.*

"I promise." I place my other hand over hers, "I'll do everything I can to end this."

"Good." She pulls her hand away. "Because when I get out of this hospital, I want to go to the aquarium, and I'm certainly not going by myself."

I nod my head, a smile stuck on my face. She smiles back at me, but her eyes are full of worry. The door opens and in steps her dad and a nurse.

"I'm sorry but visiting time is almost over," the nurse tells us.

"That's fine," I look back to Zoë. "We were just finishing up here."

I stand up and make my way to the door. Zoë's dad nods to me and makes his way to Zoë's side. I stop at the door when I hear Zoë's voice call out.

"Aaron." I look back at her. "Please stay safe. I don't know what I would do if I lost you."

I give her a final smile and nod of my head, before stepping out into the hallway.

I promise, Zoë.

***

I catch a bus back home. By the time I arrive, the sun has begun to set. Hunger and exhaustion tear at me as I walk into the front door. My mom greets me with a hug. Chloe greets me with a forced smile and Jake cries out with joy.

My mom has dinner ready for me. My favorite, spaghetti and meatballs. After helping myself to three plates. I play with Jake for a while, his action figures end up beating mine in the end. Chloe takes him away and prepares him for bed. I sit on the couch silently with my mom until she returns. Once she does, I tell them what about to happen.

"I'm going to go to sleep now." I look to the two of them. A mixture of concern and fear rests on their faces. "One way or another, this will be the last time I ever have these nightmares."

"You say that like you're about to die," Chloe challenges.

"That's because I might," I admit.

"Stop it!" my mom demands. "You are not going to die. There has to be some other way."

"There isn't." I tell her. "Either I manage to make Finnan end whatever pact he has with the Dullahan or..."

"You die," Chloe finishes. "And Jake not long after you."

I nod my head slowly. My heart races as I think about what might be coming next.

"Why is this happening?" My mom asks. "What does this Finnan guy get out of all this?"

"I don't know," I answer. "The Dullahan isn't allowed to tell me. But I will find out."

I stand up, my mom and sister follow me. They both pull me into a hug, crying as they do. I don't. For the first time since all this started, I'm not scared or sad. Not even anger burns away inside me. I just feel grim determination.

One way or another. This ends tonight!

I pull away from my mom and sister and start to head for my bathroom. I shut the door behind me and strip off my clothes and take on final look at myself in the mirror. My face is the most noticeable thing. The left side a dark, leathery scar. My left eye gleams sky blue in the light of the room. On my right cheek, a small cut has healed into a small scar. Where the Dullahan had struck me during our first encounter.

My chest was a mess with two long, deep scars stretching across it. More scars littered my stomach where the vulture sank its talons into me and where I'd been stabbed by that demon. My legs were wrapped in more scars, as though I had reversed tan lines. My back was covered is lashes from the Dullahan's whip. My hands, although wrapped in bandages tingled as though they had fallen asleep. I could still feel the scars underneath the wrappings.

Just one more night.

I step into the shower and let the warm water fall over me. As it does, I think over everything that has happened these past weeks.

I've almost died a dozen times. I've met my father, who in turn saved my life. Zoë admitted that she knew I loved her. I met my great aunt Claudia. Zoë went missing. I beat Deacon almost to death. I was trapped by Deacon. I attacked a guy at a bar. I killed Deacon. I almost got Zoë killed.

So much has happened. So much chaos and near-death experiences. But somehow, I feel like it all was for a good thing. I can say I'm more confident than I was. Zoë and I are now closer. I've met family members I didn't have the chance to know beforehand. But more than anything, I've learned to appreciate life more.

That's for certain. If I survive tonight. I'm going to live an entirely different kind of life.

I finish taking my shower. I throw on a pair shorts and make myself comfortable in my bed. I take a final look at my phone screen. At the picture of me and Zoë at the aquarium. And with a sigh, close my eyes.

***

The air around me is still. I look around and find myself in the middle of a library. The sun shines through a large window to my left. I look down and find Dante's Inferno open on the table before me. I chuckle as I close it. Standing up, I focus on the walls of the library. I picture them breaking away like the white room I was in.

Hopefully outside, there isn't the cold void of space.

My eyes open to find myself now in the center on a small town. To my right is a small drug store. To my left, the setting sun shines in my eyes. Before me, a movie theater. In big bold letters, it reads: **Now showing: Headless Horsman**

I snicker at that. I look back to my left. The sun shines fiercely in my eyes, and I hold my hand up to block it. As I peek through my fingers, I see the silhouette of a man walking towards me. I lower my hands as I prepare to fight.

A brilliant flash of light fills the space between me and the Dullahan. The amulet around my neck once more provides a shield to protect me from the dangers of the Dullahan. As fast as before, another strike from his whip collides with the air just before me, the amulet burns hot and the smell of my burning shirt fills my nose.

This continues for a moment, strike after strike as the Dullahan's whip slams into a shield of pure energy around me. As this continues, I feel the amulet grow even hotter, so hot that it begins to hurt. I know now that this can't go one for much longer. I can't win this fight of attrition. And I can't waste my time with the Dullahan.

I must find Finnan!

But before I can think of a way to fight back against the Dullahan, the whip slams into the shield of energy one final time, and I watch the shield shatter and fade into nothing before my eyes. Another flash of the Dullahan's whip and my vision goes black. A searing pain rips through my eyes. The thunderous crack of the Dullahan's whip tears through the air seconds after, knocking me backwards.

I hit the ground and the air is knocked out of my lungs. I gasp for air desperately. My vision still black I am unable to see the Dullahan snap his whip at me again, nearly ripping my arm off. With my other arm, I grip the amulet tightly. I try to focus on it, to make it do something. But it has grown cold.

"A useful tool," the Dullahan says, "it certainly helped keep you alive longer than I'd expected."

The wind starts to rip and torrent around me. Once more I feel unbelievable pain as the Dullahan's whip rips through my left leg, ripping away with it most of my thigh.

"But effective as it may be, it cannot stop me forever. Like a mountain against a river, it was only a matter of time before its power wore out."

I try to focus on healing but again am stunned as the Dullahan's whip slices open my stomach. I cry out in pain and focus on the ground beneath me. Although I can't see it, I can feel it. I imagine it splitting open, swallowing me whole.

"You're not running from me anymore, Mr. Ward," the Dullahan tells me, "This ends tonight."

I feel his spine whip wrap around my other leg. With a mighty tug, I am pulled towards the Dullahan. Unable to see, unable to hear, and unable to fight. I feel all hope leave me. An icy cold rock sinks in my stomach. The cold begins to spread all throughout my body. As I come to a stop in front of what I assume is the Dullahan, I prepare for death.

"You better not die on me, Aaron!" Zoë's voice screams in my ears.

"Get up sweetie!" My mom's voice rings out.

"You promised nothing would happen to Jake!" Chloe cries out.

The screams of hundreds of people slowly start to fill my ears. Zoë, my mom, Chloe, Aunt Claudia, my dad, Mr. St. John, Brian, and more. My ears feel as though they are bleeding. But with the pain, comes silence. No more wind, no more voices. Just the distant sounds of my own breathing.

Time seems to slow down. As I lay on the ground, waiting for death. I feel every second pass like a grain of sand through the hourglass. Each second stretching out into hours. The silence is deafening. I fear as though this will last for an eternity. Then I hear it. The dull dragging of The Dullahan's whip against the ground. Although I can't see, I can picture what's happening. The Dullahan is preparing to bring his whip down on my head.

The amulet in my hand warms up. The blood in my hand begins to boil as I clutch it tightly. And with a desperate scream I hold the amulet in the air to where I imagine the Dullahan's whip to be. As the two objects collide, a roar of fury and agony fill my ears from the Dullahan as I imagine golden flames engulfing him once more. The amulet in my hand explodes into dust.

Run!

Once more I think about the ground. I envision is splitting open like a giant mouth, swallowing me whole before closing forever. I picture rapids below the ground carrying me towards the sea. Towards Finnan. Within an instant, the ground opens beneath me and I fall helplessly. I cannot see. Cannot move. I bounce off the side off the cavern I've created and start tumbling downwards.

The Dullahan's screams of fury shake the air around me. Thunder bellows down towards me. But still I fall, away from the Dullahan and his whip. Hopefully, towards Finnan.

***

As I fall, I start to force my body to heal. My eyes regrow in their sockets. Not that they are of much use, as the canyon I've created seems to be a bottomless pit of darkness. My leg and stomach stitch themselves back together and my arm fuses into place. I feel as though I've just stuck my arm in an oven. But soon enough, I'm back in working order.

Wouldn't be a good night's sleep with a few new scars for the collection.

Out of nowhere I slam into water. My back cracks and for what I pray is the final time the air is ripped away from my lungs. The water twists and turns around me, pulling me deeper into its abyss. I sink as though my feet were tied to a boulder. Faster and faster, I am pulled downwards.

As fast as the water appeared I find myself breaking its surface. No longer sinking through its dark depths but instead wading in a vast, empty sea. I look around in all directions, waiting to see Finnan's ship. But I am dismayed to find myself utterly alone.

Something brushes against my foot. Looking down, I nearly faint as I see a massive shadow pass below me. Panic threatens to take over, and I'm about to start swimming madly in the other direction. Frustration at my own cowardice steels me. And I look down at the massive shadow below me.

It brushes against my leg once more. I picture a large boat rising out of the water, lifting me to safety. I wait for a few seconds and instead of miraculous safety in the hands of a boat, I feel the shadow take hold of my leg. The creature, whatever it is, sinks its teeth into my calf and I'm instantly pulled back under the water.

The creature drags me further into the murky depths. I struggle in vain as the creature's jaws clamp down painfully on my leg. Seeing no escape, I will a long knife into existence. My right-hand grips onto it tightly as I rapidly sink. My vision murky and dark, I feel with my free hand for the creature. When I find what I believe to be its nose, I plunge my knife as deep as I can into it.

The creature wails in pain and releases my leg. I'm set spinning in the current the creature leaves behind as it continues its course downwards. Once I regain control over my body, I start to swim upwards. I swim faster than I ever have before. The light of the surface races towards me.

Hope wells in my chest. A dozen feet from the water's surface, my own curiosity forces me to look downwards.

    Below me, racing up after me, is a large shadow. I scream, what little air I had left in my lungs leaving me. The shadow rapidly approaches me. I look back up and find myself inches away from the surface. Just before I can reach it, the shadow crashes into me and lifts me high into the air.

Chapter 18

I slam onto the wooden deck of a ship. Water droplets rain down all around me as I gag and cough on the salty water. My leg burns madly, forcing me to sit up and take stock of myself. The area around my leg is a mess or shredded skin and muscle. Bone pokes through in some places and the deck runs red with my blood. Placing both my hands over the mess that is my leg, I focus. After about a minute, my leg returns to normal.

Why is it that it looks fine now? It's just gonna be a massive scar when I wake up anyway.

"Good lord, laddie!" Finnan's voice calls out to me. "You sure are good at being rescued by me!"

I look up from my restored leg and see Finnan walking towards me. His long brown hair tied back into a ponytail. A new scar has appeared over his right eye. From the looks of it I'd say it came from the Dullahan.

"Finnan." I reply coldly.

"Ok, savin' yer thanks for later, eh?" Finnan quips.

"I'm not thanking you for shit, you motherfucker!" I shout at him.

Finnan pauses, only a couple feet in front of me. The look on his face is one of shaded curiosity. Finally, with a sigh and a click of his tongue, he speaks.

"He told you."

"Yeah, he told me." My jaw creaks as I clench it.

"And what exactly did he say to you?"

"That you made a deal with a demon," I spit at him. "That you damned your entire fucking bloodline to being that bastard's food for centuries!"

Finnan is silent. A pensive look on his face. His eyes are dark, malice gleaming within them.

"Why?" I ask him. "What did you get out of it?"

"Everything," Finnan says coldly.

"Everything? What the fuck did you sell your families souls for!" I scream at him, rage boiling my blood. "Was anything you ever told me true?"

"You really think the truth will help you?"

"Yes, I fucking do!" I scream at him. The air around us slowly grows colder over the course of our conversation.

Finnan sighs with frustration. "Fine." He walks over to the edge of the ship and leans against it. I follow him, keeping my distance.

"Start talking." I demand.

Finnan nods his head. "I didn't lie to ya when I said I didn't want to be king. The life of a king is either boring politics or never-ending war. The fear that yer own people will seek to remove yer head from yer shoulders. It's exhausting."

"Stop wasting my time!" I shout at him. The sky above begins to grow darker as massive storm clouds form.

"I never cared for much. So long as I had a belly full of ale and meat, a sword wet with blood from a recent battle, and a beautiful woman around my cock."

I roll my eyes at the sly smile that spreads across Finnan's face.

"I never craved power," he goes on. "Or fame. Not even wealth mattered to me. So long as I had those three things, I was the happiest man in all of Europe."

"So, what changed?" I ask. "What was so big that you destroyed our family for it?"

"Aoibhe." Finnan looks to the deck, a wistful look about him. "She was the most beautiful woman I had ever seen. Of course, being the king's daughter, she certainly should've been. The moment I set my eyes on her, I knew I would do anything to have her. I'd kill any man, slay any beast, make any deal..." He looks up to me, a glint of evil shining in his eyes.

"So, you damned your entire family line, your brothers and sisters, your nieces and nephews, your own children, for a woman?" I feel sick at the thought.

"I never had children," Finnan corrects. "Would you? Knowing what ya know now."

"All this, for a woman?" I shake my head in disbelief.

"Not just any woman lad, the perfect woman." He pushes off the side of the ship, taking a step towards me. "No other more beautiful. No other more kind. No other gentler."

"But why? Why let this go on any longer?" I ask him. "You're dead, both of you are dead. Why not end the pact with the Dullahan?"

"The pact I made with the Dullahan states that not only will I have the hand in marriage of the woman I desire, but that I shall spend eternity on an endless sea. Living a life of ceaseless adventure with her at my side."

"Her at your side?" I echo, my hands starting to shake from the cold.

The sun and sky now completely covered by thick, black storm clouds. Finnan takes another step towards me.

"Aoibhe!" he calls out. "Come to me, my love!"

At the back of the ship, the captains' quarters are underneath the upper deck where the ships wheel is. The door to the cabin opens and a young woman emerges. Her hair black as the sky on a moonless night. Her eyes, as green as the grassy fields in late spring. Her flawless white skin shined even in the shadows of the storm. When she reached the two of us, she takes Finnan's hands and pulls herself in, kissing him passionately. As their lips part, she looks to me.

"So, this is your sister's descendant?" She looks me up and down. "He seems sad, does he not?"

"What the fuck am I looking at?" I say, shocked at the sight before me.

"Aaron, this is my lovely wife, Aoibhe." He turns to look at me, "Aoibhe, meet Aaron."

"Hello, Aaron." She smiles warmly, her eyes soft and alluring as she stares at me.

"Finnan, what…" I stammer.

"You see now why I could never let the pact end?" Finnan asks. "How could I ever let what I have with her end?"

As I stare at Aoibhe, an idea strikes me. "Aoibhe, do you know what Finnan has done to me?"

"I know about his deal with the Dullahan, yes," she says. "I'd say I was sorry, but how could I be? He's sacrificed so much, just to be with me."

She titles her head and rests it against Finnan's chest. He puts his arms around her, holding her softly. Anger begins to burn in my chest.

These selfish bastards!

"Finnan," I grunt. "You need to end your pact with the Dullahan, now."

"If ye had Zoë here, right now. Offering for you to spend eternity with her on the open sea. Would ya pass at that just because a few people ye don't know or care for have to die?"

"Without question." I ball up my fists. "Because the Zoë I know would never be able to look at me if I did."

"Then she's a fool," Aoibhe speaks softly. "Who'd throw away an eternal life of happiness and adventure for those who wouldn't do the same for her?"

"Don't you dare talk about her!" I scream at Aoibhe.

In an instant a whip made of human spines appears in my hand. Without thinking of what I am doing, I crack the whip at Aoibhe. Finnan grabs the end of the whip, snatching it out of the air just before it strikes Aoibhe. A mask of fury rests on his face.

"That was a mistake!" The whip is set aflame in my hand.

I shout out in painful surprise, dropping the whip the moment the flames lick my hand. On both sides of me, two shadowy members of Finnan's crew appear. They take ahold of both my arms and hold me in place. I fight against them, to no avail.

"What are you going to do Finnan? Kill me?" I laugh obnoxiously at him.

"I'm certainly tempted, too," he snarls.

"But you can't, can you?" I laugh more. "Cause if you do, then all the Dullahan has to do is kill a little kid and your eternal paradise ends!"

"You think death is the worst thing that can happen to you?" Finnan steps forwards, his face an inch away from mine. "The things I could do to you would drive you mad!"

I smile coyly at his threat. "Like what?"

He smiles, a mad glint in his eyes. "Look and see what awaits you." He looks to the shadows that hold me in place.

I look to my left and see the shadow of a man. His body pure black, waves of purple ripple across the surface of his skin. I look up to his face and feel my heart jump to my lungs.

His face, all but buried under pure darkness, is that of my dad. His eyes lock onto mine, and they scream out with pain. I look to my right and see that the other shadow that holds me in place is that of my cousin, Brian. His eyes are equally full of torment.

"What…?" I stammer, my throat dry. "What did you do to them?"

"Like I said," Finnan grins, "There are worst things than death."

"But I thought…"

"The Dullahan killed them?" Finnan cuts me off. "Well, he did. And he ate their souls as he so often does. But you see, it seems I was right about the soul having multiple pieces."

"So, you enslaved my family?" I stare in disbelief at Finnan. "What kind of monster are you?"

"I didn't enslave anyone." Finnan takes Aoibhe's hand. "As I said, the soul is made of several parts. The Dullahan feeds off the soul, that's true, but not all of it. You see, the shadow of a person is a part of their soul. But it's also their history. Their legacy on the world. A footprint even. The Dullahan either can't or doesn't eat this, leaving it to wander this world aimlessly. No purpose, no meaning." Finnan strokes Aoibhe's cheek softly. "But I gave them one."

"By enslaving them on your ship?"

"Well, I needed a crew, didn't I?" Finnan chuckles.

"You're mad." Snow begins to fall on us. "You are absolutely fucking insane."

"Even if I am, what does it matter?" Finnan steps towards me once more.

Rage has slowly been pooling within me. With Finnan's words, it spills over and drives me to seeing red. Using whatever power I have; I throw off the shadows of my dad and cousin. Finnan stands in shock as I slam myself into him. Snow is beginning to fall heavily down and the sky rumbles with thunder off in the distance.

I push Finnan into the side of the ship and start to punch him repeatedly. He raises his hands to guard his face and I waste no time trying to crush his ribs. Desperately, Finnan wraps his arms around me and tries to pin my arms to my sides. With a scream of fury, I push Finnan over the side of the ship and he takes me with him.

The ocean has frozen beneath us. The two of us slam into its icy surface, separating as we hit the ground. Anger forces me up off the ice and I proceed to tackle a winded Finnan. He holds up his arm and gets me into a headlock, pinning my face into the ice. The heat radiating from our bodies gives me an idea and I force the ice directly beneath us to melt.

We both fall through the ice into the freezing cold water below. Finnan tries to swim for the surface, and I grab ahold of him, dragging him down deeper into the water. He elbows me in the face, desperately trying to dislodge me from him. I picture a knife in my hand and stab it into his side.

Finnan's cries of pain reverberate through the water, and he manages to finally push me off him. He races off towards the surface of the water while I start to sink deeper into the abyss below. My head rings from the cold and all over I feel my body start to shut down. I look up and watch Finnan pull himself out of the water and the flame of anger reignites within me.

I'll kill you!

The ice above me splinters and cracks into several large pieces as a meteor smashes into the sea. Finnan's ship shakes and groans as another meteor crashes down from the sky. I ignore the pain throughout my body and start to swim back up to the surface. My head breaches the surface of the water. Beside me is a large chunk of ice and I swim over to it.

Once I've pulled myself out of the water, I look around for Finnan. The water below heaves and shakes as more meteors rain down. I stumble; in the corner of my eye, I see Finnan making his way slowly back to his ship. A ladder has been lowered for him and at its top, Aoibhe looks down at him.

"Finnan!" I scream, the ocean exploding behind me as the largest meteor yet collides with the sea.

Finnan stops running for his ship. He turns to look at me and for the first time, I see fear in his eyes.

Coward!

"Aaron!" Finnan shouts over the many explosions as more meteors hit the ocean. "This won't fix anything! You can't kill me!"

Roaring with hatred, I start to run towards him. I jump from ice sheet to ice sheet, determined to get him before he reaches his ship. I watch as he gets closer, Aoibhe cheering him on.

I want that ship and that bitch gone!

A meteor slams into the side of the ship. Finnan cries out in anguish as the ship tilts to its side, the ladder falling to the water below. Another meteor hits the ship, cracking it in half. Fires rage all across it as it begins to sink beneath the water. Finnan comes to a stop just a few feet from where the ladder was.

"Aoibhe!" he cries.

I scream as I charge into him, sending him flying through the air and back into the water. His head breaches the surface as he gasps for air. I flick my wrist and force a whirlpool to appear, sucking him back under the water. I stand there for a moment, that meteors still falling with the snow around me as I watch Finnan drown.

A flash of orange light rockets through the water and a large explosion blows apart my whirlpool. My feet go out from underneath me as the shockwave hits the sheet of ice I stand on. I start to pick myself up when Finnan rockets out of the water, landing right in front of me.

"Aaron!" Finnan screams "Do you have any idea what you've done?"

"I killed a dead woman!" I scream back, the sky exploding as more meteors rain down. "And I'll kill you, too!"

We both scream and charge each other. We send ourselves spinning to the ground as we collide, and Finnan manages to get on top of me. He grunts with effort as he starts to beat me senseless.

"I saved your life!" Finn screams, each word interrupted by a punch. "I kept you alive! And this is how you repay me!"

I roll Finnan over, now I'm on top of him. I start to punch him as well. With each time my fist connects with his face, the sky erupts with thunder and lightning. A blizzard rages around us and meteors continue to smash into the ocean.

"You saved me?" I scream down at Finnan. "You damned me! You damned my entire family! All for some fucking princess!"

Finnan musters all his strength and throws me off him. I hit the ground, the back of my head bouncing off the ice. Spots dance in my vision and my ears ring violently. As I try to pick myself up off the ice, Finnan appears above me.

"I did what any man would do!" he cries out, before slamming his knee down on me.

I throw up water. My vision begins to spin as Finnan starts to beat me once more.

"You think I need you?" he laughs at me. "I can keep that nephew of yours alive. Long enough for your family to have more children. More sacrifices!"

I can't see Finnan anymore; my eyes are pooling with my own blood. What anger and energy I had are now no more than smoldering embers of a fire. Finnan's punches slam down against my skull, and I don't feel them anymore. I only hear the dull drumming of my brain bouncing off my skull.

Finnan suddenly stops hitting me. I feel as though I'm about to be delivered a final blow. When instead I hear Finnan screaming out in protest. I lift my head and rub the blood out of my eyes. My right eye is swollen shut, but the scarred tissue around my left refuses to. Through one eye, I see Finnan being held down by what I can only assume are the shadows of my dad and Brian.

"Get off of me, ya cunts!" Finnan yells at them. "I said, get off me!"

I push myself up and immediately stumble to the ground once more. I gather what little strength I have left and force myself up again. I stumble to the ground beside Finnan and stare down at him.

"Aaron!" he screams at me. "You can't kill me!"

I look up to my dad and cousin. Their eyes are locked on Finnan. What was once a look of perpetual terror and pain has now been replaced by overwhelming hatred. He strains against them, and the shadow of my dad snaps his arm in response. Finnan cries out in pain and looks back to me.

"What are you gonna do?" he screams at me. "You can't kill me! So, what are you going to do, huh!"

I lean down, pressing my mouth to Finnan's ear.

"You think death is the worst thing that can happen to you?" I whisper.

"Aaron!" he screams.

I look at him and picture the ice directly beneath him becoming shattered glass. He cries out in pain as the glass shreds his back. I stare at his hand and imagine giant nails holding him to the ice. Again, he cries out with pain as the nails appear, tearing his hands open. I look to his face, all contorted in pain. I rest my hand on the left side of his head, just over his eye. And I feel my hand ignite with flames as I burn half his face off.

Finnan's screams are drowned out as his blood pools in his throat. I take my injured hand away from his face and look down at the mutilated man. His eye has popped and oozes like a half-cooked egg. The muscle of his face is charred and black, the bones of his skull gleam white.

"There is so much more I can do." I speak softly, my words cutting through Finnan's screams. "All you have to do to stop it is to end your deal."

Finnan tries to speak but coughs instead. Flecks of his blood splatter across my face. I expect anger to ignite within me once more but am left feeling numb. I look down at Finnan's stomach and drag my finger across it. As I do, his stomach tears open. Finnan howls into the air as I rip his stomach open, tears streaming from his one good eye.

I stare down at him, ashamed and disgusted at his cries of agony. His eye stares up at me through a puddle of tears. Fear shines from it and a sickly-sweet feeling swells in my chest.

"Do you want to end your pact with the Dullahan?" I ask him.

Finnan's eye goes wide, his nostrils flaring with rapid breaths.

"You just have to say yes," I coax. "Just one word and all this ends."

Still Finnan is silent. I reach down, placing my hand directly over his chest. I stare at him, waiting for him to say something. His breathing grows faster as I extend my fingers over his chest, right above his heart.

"Last chance," I tell him.

Again, he remains silent. Clenching my jaw, I feel my hand start to burn away the flesh of Finnan's chest. He screams in horror as I slowly burrow my hand deeper into his chest. After a few seconds, I feel his beating heart throb against my hand. I stare back down at him, a stone forming in my gut.

"Yes," he whispers.

Finally!

I rip his heart out of his chest. He screams for a second before it dissolves into a desperate gasp for air. I watch as he struggles to free himself from the bed of glass.

From the nails in his hands. From under the weight of my dad and cousin's shadows. All in vain.

"Very impressive," the Dullahan's deep voice calls out above me.

I look up and see the Dullahan standing over us. His whip tied to his waist, his head in hand.

"The pact is over," I tell him.

"I know." The Dullahan sighs with relief. "Already I feel as though heavy chains have been lifted and now, I'm free to soar across the sky."

"No." Finnan groans. "No. Please."

"Silence!" the Dullahan orders.

He opens his eyes and I shut mine tightly. I feel Finnan struggle underneath me. His entire body convulsing with pain. A guttural gurgling emanates from him. Finnan struggles for several minutes like this. Until finally, he lies still. I open my eyes and look down at him. I'm surprised to see that rather than Finnan lying there on the ice before me, there is instead a shadow. The shadow of the man who damned his family for love.

"Ah, that was delicious," the Dullahan sighs.

"So, is it over?" I ask him, standing up.

As I stand, the shadows of my dad, Brian, and Finnan fade away. As do the nails and broken glass. Around us, the meteors have stopped falling and the ice slowly is reforming. The Dullahan holds his head his side, a grim look resting upon it.

"Sadly, not yet," he answers.

"What do you mean?" I prepare to run for my life. "The pact is over; you have no reason to kill me now."

"Indeed, the pact is over." He sighs. "But you see, your soul must still be eaten."

"Why?"

"Because if I do not, you will suffer a fate even worse than death at my gaze." He turns around and looks over the frozen ocean.

The clouds in the sky have disappeared. Overhead, the night sky shimmers brightly with thousands of stars. Hues of purple and pick swirl around in between them. It is beautiful.

"That's bullshit!" I scream at him. "After everything I've been through! I still have to die? Why?"

"Everything dies, with time, Aaron." He turns back to look at me. "The question isn't why, but when."

"When?"

"You have done me a great service. You have freed me from an endless prison. One I was forced to share with that monster of a man."

"You're calling him a monster?" I laugh.

"You think that just because I must consume the souls of humans that I'm a monster?" he challenges. "Do you think a cow thinks the same of you? Or what of a head of broccoli? Is a plant not alive?"

"That's different."

"Is it?" he asks. "Just because you can't hear a plant voice its protest or understand a cow doesn't mean they don't think of you as a monster."

"So, you think you're a good guy?" I scoff.

"I don't think anything of either sort," the Dullahan corrects. "I am a demon; I must eat the souls of humans to survive. I don't enjoy doing so, yet I must all the same. This makes me neither good nor evil."

"But you're still killing me even though you don't have to." I shout at him. "Finnan is gone, there is nothing forcing you to kill me."

"Oh, but there is." The Dullahan turns to face me, resting his free hand on my shoulder. "Do you not remember what I told you? Twice now you should be dead. Finnan told you that there was more than one part to your soul, did he not?"

"You're not making any sense!" I brush his hand off my shoulder.

"I have already consumed two parts of your soul," he states. "You are already half dead as a result."

I'm silent for a while.

I'm already dead?

"You will start to feel it soon. This empty feeling in your heart. As though you lost something you never knew you had. You'll go through the rest of your life with this feeling. And when the day comes that you do die, your soul with shred itself."

"Why will it do that?"

"Because part of it resides in me," the Dullahan points to his chest. "I consume but do not destroy. The souls of all I've consumed remain with me. They fuel me, for a while. And when they no longer can, I release them."

"You release them?" I question. "Then why can you release the parts of my soul you've already eaten?"

"Can you throw up half a steak and make it whole again?" he asks.

"No?"

"Neither can I with your soul. The only way you can be restored is within me."

"So, in order for me to truly die, I have to let you kill me?" I clarify.

"Yes."

I'll never see my family again? Zoë? Never feel the warmth of the sun on my face? Never play with Jake again?

"Is there any other option?" I ask.

"There is not." His eyes twitch. "However, I don't need to do this now."

"Wait, you don't?" My eyes go wide, hope fluttering in my chest.

"I don't need to kill you immediately" he clears his throat. "It can be put off for a time."

I'm not going to die right this second?

"For how long?"

"About twenty years."

"That's it? Twenty years?" I exclaim. "That's not enough!"

"Any longer and the risk of you dying from some other way increases greatly. It would be a great risk for both of us."

"Both of us?"

"Well, yes," he chuckles. "If your soul was to destroy itself, it would certainly hurt me. Not enough to kill me I don't think but enough to where I don't want it to happen."

"So, you'll give me twenty years. But then you'll kill me?"

"I promise, it will be painless," he assures. "As well as I promise, not a single other member of your family will ever be hunted by me ever again."

I look up to the sky again.

"Will I stop having these nightmares?"

"Yes. You well not see this world again until the day you die."

Twenty years to live the best life I can. Is that enough? Twenty years to spend with my family. With Zoë. I can watch Jake grow up and graduate high school. I can be with Zoë, maybe I still have a chance with her. I can be happy. But then...

"Ok." I hold out my hand. "I accept."

The Dullahan shakes my hand. For the first time since these nightmares began, I'm completely calm. The stars start to shine brighter in the sky. And the last thing I hear before I wake up, is the thundering of hooves on ice.

Chapter 19

I stare at Zoë across the yard. She's talking with Chloe. Her hair is now styled short. But besides her hair, she looks no different, as though time has not touched her. Chloe's red hair is long, reaching down to her waist. In her arms is her second child, another son. She'd found a better man this time around. I was certainly happy for her.

My daughter, Bella, is at Zoë's side, holding her hand. She's only five years old. Her short brown hair is unkempt and sticks out like she'd just been electrocuted. Her gray eyes stare emptily at the grass.

She's bored.

I look over and see Jake, now all grown up. He got tall, too, and muscular. Star of the basketball team, he certainly was popular in high school. He'd graduated a few years ago and was currently going to Northwestern University on a sports scholarship. We were all so proud when we heard the news.

My mom sits beside my aunt Katrina and aunt Claudia. My mom and Aunt Katrina had gotten older, but still seemed so full of love and life. Aunt Katrina remarried a few years after Brian's death, and now was a proud step mom of twins. Although she still grieved what she'd lost, she never forgot how to love and live.

Aunt Claudia was ancient now, the type of old where people seem to shrink. Her hair is pure white and short. But her mind seemed to grow stronger around family. She says something to my mom and aunt Katrina and the trio burst out into laughter.

Zoë's dad sits down at a table, quietly conversing with another family member. I started working for him at his workshop about a year after the nightmares ended. He was ecstatic when I asked for his blessing to marry Zoë. Ever since Bella was born, he spends as much time as he can over at our house. He loves babysitting.

All my friends and family are gathered around my backyard in celebration. I walk around my house in silence for a while before heading out to greet them all. I stare at the many pictures that aligned the walls.

Zoë is an avid photographer, always making sure to take as many pictures as she can of our many travels. When we started dating after she had gotten out of the hospital, I decided that the two of us needed to get away from the city. So, the day after graduation, I took her to see the Grand Canyon. After that adventure, it became a regular occurrence. Eventually, we found ourselves living on the road for a year, seeing everything worth seeing in the country. We even went to Alaska at one point.

Our vacations stopped when we learned that Zoë was pregnant. I was terrified, of course. After everything I went through, how could I think to bring a child into this world? My fears were only slightly subdued when I learned we were having a girl. But as time has gone by, I feel more at peace than ever before.

I check the calendar for the millionth time today. June 19th, 2039. Zoë's birthday. And the last day I would be alive. I was scared for a while. I didn't want to tell anyone. I wanted to cry, it had to be her birthday.

I stare at a picture of my family. My arm is stretched around Zoë's waist, pulling her close. I take notice of my beard, which is patchy in some places but suits me nicely, I am often told. My numerous scars have faded considerably well over the course of my life, to the point that if they weren't pointed out to you, you would hardly even notice them. The outlier being my cloudy blue eyes.

After being blinded by the Dullahan in my last nightmare, my other eye turned blue. They suited me, made me seem more handsome, Zoë often joked. But they are a cold reminder every morning when I'd look in the mirror of what I'd been through.

In another picture, Zoë is holding a newborn Bella in her arms. Bella's head is held up by Zoë's hand. Zoë's smile shines across her face, making her look even more beautiful than I thought possible. Again, I want to cry, but cannot.

I haven't been able to cry since I awoke from my last nightmare. There were other things I started to notice, too. Like the heavy weight I felt on my chest all the time, as though I had several bricks laying on me. As well as a deep chill that regularly would run down my spine, like someone was dragging an ice cube down my back.

I know was it is. As the Dullahan had said, I'd lost half my soul in fighting him. Things were never going to be the same as a result. But if half my soul was the price I had to pay to live the life I've lived, I'd do it again.

"Daddy!" Bella's voice sings out.

I step into the living room and see Bella's head poking in from the sliding glass door that leads outside. She smiles as she sees me.

"What is it, lovebug?" I return the smile, making my way over to the door.

"Mommy said to come get you."

"Oh, did she now?" I open the door and scoop her up off the ground. She giggles as I shut the door behind me, stepping into the backyard.

"Mommy!" she calls out.

Zoë is still talking with Chloe. She turns around as I approach her, Bella smiling gleefully in my arms.

"I found him!" Bella tells her mom.

"You did!" Zoë takes her from my arms, "I knew you could."

I look at Chloe. I feel like saying something to her. Her eyes lock onto mine and for a moment, sadness wells within them. Before either of us say anything, she smiles and leaves, her son asleep in her arms. I look back to Zoë and see a similar look on her face.

"What?" I ask her.

"Nothing," she says, setting Bella down. "Just making sure you are ok."

"I'm fine, honey."

"I know you are. Just, I worry."

"And I love you for it." I lean in and kiss her. As I pull away, I whisper happy birthday.

"Thanks." She forces a smile. "I'm surprised by how many came."

"Well, what can I say. I am pretty popular." I suppress a laugh as she gives me the stink eye.

"What, you think this is your party?"

"Well, I don't know why else all these people would be here." I smile at her.

"Oh no, just you wait till it's your…" her voice trails off.

"Aaron!" My mom appears from behind me. "Is there going to be any cake?"

"Oh, yes!" Zoë exclaims. "Let me go get it."

"No, no, no!" My mom argues. "It's your birthday, you shouldn't be getting your own cake!"

"No, its fine." Zoë looks at me. "Let Aaron relax today."

As she walks away, I feel a chill run down my spine again. Followed by a pain in my heart as I watch the woman I love walk away. My mom turns to face me.

"How are you doing?" she asks.

"I'm fine, Mom." I groan. "Really, I am."

"Ok." She holds her hands up. "I won't ask again."

"Thank you."

My mom swirls a drink in her hand for a moment. Then she pulls me into a hug.

"I'm going to miss you," she whispers in my ear.

I hug her tightly. I will tears to appear, but to no avail. I still cannot cry.

***

The party ends. Most of the guests have left already. Except for Chloe's family and my mom. Zoë takes Bella away for a bath and then bed, leaving me with my family.

"So," my mom says, holding back tears. "This is it."

"I guess so," I reply.

Chloe turns to her husband, who holds their second son in his hands. She asks them to go wait in the car while she says goodbye. He nods and tells me goodnight before leaving. Jake goes to follow before I stop him, pulling him into a hug.

"Hey, just in case I haven't told you already today, I'm proud of you."

"Thanks, Uncle Aaron." He smiles, his voice deeper than mine.

"Now go on, get." I shove him playfully. "You need a good night's rest for that game you've got tomorrow."

"Yes, sir," he laughs.

I watch as he walks away. Thanking God that he won't ever have to go through what I did. I look back to my mom and sister. Both are holding back tears, and I pull them both into a large hug.

"Please, don't cry," I tell them.

Chloe pushes me away. "How are we not supposed to cry, Aaron?"

"Look, I know this isn't easy. But there isn't anything we can do about it," I declare.

"You're not even trying to do anything about it!" Chloe argues.

"That's enough." My mom puts her hand on Chloe's shoulder. "You know that isn't true. The fact that he's here now is proof of how hard he fought to stay."

"How are you so calm about this?" Chloe asks her.

"Because I got twenty years with my son that I had begun to think I never would've." She sighs. "I've made peace with what will happen. Just as he has. Just as Zoë has."

I stand there in silence for a while. I didn't know what to say. All I could to was memories the details of their faces. I wanted to remember them for as long as I could. Finally, Chloe wiped the tears away from her eyes and started for the door. She stops just before closing it, looking back towards me.

"I'll miss you," she sobs.

"I'll miss you, too." I smile warmly.

It's best the last thing she sees me doing is smiling.

Chloe turns back around and closes the door behind her. I look back to my mom, who pulls me into another hug.

"I'm sorry," I sob. Although still no tears.

"Don't you be sorry." She pulls away from me. "You did everything you could. You stopped a monster and survived what generations of people before you never could. And I am so proud of you."

"And now you'll have to bury your son." I hang my head. "All because I wasn't good enough."

"You stop that." She grabs my chin, lifting my head to be eye level with her. "You did more than good, you did great. You survived a hell no other person on this planet could've. And you did it for your family. For your nephew and for Zoë. You did great, and you lived a great life! Now, it's time for it to end." Her last words heavy with sadness as she forces them out of her mouth.

I pull her in for a final hug. One that lasts for what feels like hours. When we part, she looks at me and with a smile, makes her way for the door. As the door swings open, she looks over her shoulder, taking one last look at her son.

"I love you."

"I love you, too." I smile at her.

Tears start to fall down her cheek as she turns around and steps through the doorway, closing the door behind her. My chest for the first time in twenty years feels light. And I hate it.

I feel hollow.

I take one final look around my living room. And slowly make my way to my daughter's bedroom. Where inside I find my beautiful wife tucking Bella into bed.

"Hi Daddy," Bella calls out.

"Hey there, lovebug." I walk over and sit on the opposite side of the bed from Zoë. "I just came by to say goodnight."

"Goodnight, Daddy." She smiles.

I lean forwards and plant a kiss on her forehead. Zoë does the same and we both go to leave the room. Bella then calls out to me.

"You didn't check for monsters!"

With a chuckle, I make my way over and check both her closet and under her bed for monsters. After I'm done, I tell her there aren't any. I kiss her goodnight once more and leave her room, checking for one last time that her nightlight is on.

I slowly close the door behind me. I press my back against the wall and feel despair wash over me. I want to hold Bella as she falls asleep in my arms once more. I want to read her a bedtime story. Listen to her talk about her day. More than anything else, I want to cry. But my eyes remain dry.

With a deep sigh, I make my way for my bedroom. As I enter, I find a nude Zoë waiting for me. I close the door slowly behind me as I stare in awe at her. Her supple breasts called to me from edge of the room. Her soft, smooth skin begged for a gentle caress. And the hunger in her eyes told me that I was taking too long in greeting her.

I quickly tore my clothes off and climbed into bed beside her. Her lips met mine in a fury of love and lust. Her tongue danced with mine in each other's mouths. My hands were glued to her body, heat radiating from every inch of her. And for time, I forgot all about the weight on my chest. I forget about the ceaseless chill that dragged down my spine. I thought of nothing but Zoë.

***

We make love for as long as we possibly can. But eventually, our bodies grow tired and weak. We both lay in the bed beside each other, our chests heaving with breath. I look to her and feel once more my heart flutter in chest. She looks at me and I see that oh so familiar look of sadness and anger.

"That was amazing!" I gush.

"Yeah, it was," she agrees.

The room is silent except for our heavy breathing. I continue to stare at her while she looks up the ceiling. The moonlight shines down on us from our window.

"I assume that wasn't birthday sex though, was it?" I ask.

"What do you think it was?" she looks back to me.

"Goodbye?"

"Mhm." She blinks her eyes slowly. Her steel gray eyes like silver in the moonlight.

"You know I don't want to go. Right?"

"I know." She nods her head. "I wanted to be angry at you. Scream and yell, throw stuff at you. I wanted to explode."

"What stopped you?"

"Your mom. She and I have been talking about this day for the last year. Preparing. She helped me realize that you did everything you could. I knew that you'd done a lot already. Back then, with Deacon and the Dullahan, surviving so much. Doing everything you could to stay alive, to save me. She helped me understand that it's because of everything you did that we're here now. That I've lived this wonderful life. I have Bella and my dad. I have friends and family that care for me." She pauses, her eyes looking deep into mine. "I had you."

I lean forwards and plant a kiss on her lips. I pull away and open my eyes to see her still staring at me.

"I wish I didn't have to go." I lament. "But if I don't, I don't know what will happen when I do. We might never see each other ever again."

"I know." She sighs. "Any regrets?"

I smile and look up to the ceiling. I look back on my life. By family. My battle with Finnan and the numerous ones with the Dullahan beforehand. Then I thought off all the days I spent with Zoë. Before we were together.

"Only that I didn't tell you sooner how I felt."

Zoë chuckles. She leans over and pulls me into a final kiss. As our lips part, I hear her whisper:

"I love you."

Epilogue

The sky is a flurry of colors. Pinks and purples, yellows and blues all radiate from the setting sun. The open water calmly laps at my feet, the sand beneath me soft and warm. The air is cool and refreshing, the smell of lilacs wafting through it.

"Hell of a final view," I say, looking behind me to see the Dullahan.

"I figured it would be something nice to see before you went," he replies.

"Twenty years to the day." I clench my jaw. "You certainly are punctual."

"When I make a deal, I keep it," he states calmly.

"So, this is it. The end of the line."

"The start of something more," the Dullahan corrects.

"Oh? What happens next?"

"That's not for me to say," he tells me. "But I can assure you, you will see Zoë and your daughter again one day."

I nod my head, relieved to hear my worst fear won't be coming true.

"Ok then." I take a final look at the sunset. "I'm ready."

"Any final words?"

"None that need to be said." I look back to the Dullahan.

With a nod of his head, he raises it up to meet me at eye level. My heart beats furiously in my chest. The

Dullahan's eyes open and I feel everything fade away in brilliant white light.

THE END

Made in the USA
Columbia, SC
30 May 2024

36411725R00155